LAST HUNT

Also by Luke Short
in Thorndike Large Print

Sunset Graze

And the Wind Blows Free

Ambush

Play a Lone Hand

The Bounty Guns

The Branded Man

The Guns of Hanging Lake

The Man on the Blue

Also by Luke Short
in Thorndike Large Print

Sunset Graze

And the Wind Blows Free

Ambush

Play a Lone Hand

The Bounty Guns

The Branded Man

The Guns of Hanging Lake

The Man on the Blue

e Production Review Committee of N.A.V.H.
has found this book to meet its criteria
for large type publications.

LAST HUNT

LAST HUNT

LUKE SHORT

Thorndike Press • Thorndike, Maine

Library of Congress Cataloging in Publication Data:

Short, Luke, 1908-1985.
   Last hunt / Luke Short.
   p. cm.
   ISBN 0-89621-958-5 (alk. paper : lg. print)
   1. Large type books. I. Title.
[PS3513.L68158L37   1990]   89-48687
813'.54--dc20   CIP

Thorndike Press Large Print editon published in 1990 by arrangement with H. N. Swanson, Inc. Agency.

Cover design by Cynthia Bowen.

This book is printed on acid-free, high opacity paper. ∞

LAST HUNT

LAST TRAIT

I

John and Sam Lillard, father and son, and partners in the law firm of Lillard and Lillard, were preceded out of the Grafton County district courtroom by Mrs. Lola Geary, who had received her divorce some three minutes ago. Both men were wearing overcoats over their dark business suits and were carrying hats against the raw October weather outside.

Mrs. Geary was a lean and beautiful young woman of twenty-four with sand-blond hair that matched her expensive polo coat; on her face was a faint, almost enigmatic smile of triumph. It could have been contagious, for when she stopped in the corridor both her attorneys to whom she turned smiled too — the white-haired, blocky John, and the balding, stocky Sam.

"Well, that's over and done with," Lola Geary said.

"Judge Overman was with you all the way, Lola," John Lillard observed.

Sam saw the tears growing in Lola's blue eyes and he said, "No need for that, Lola. The

7

time for crying is past."

"Oh, I know, Sam," Lola said quietly. "It's just that it's the end of something. It never was any good, but it's the end."

Suddenly she looked past John's shoulder and Sam saw her expression alter slightly.

"Here's Bill," she said.

The two men turned to regard Bill Geary, who was approaching them. He was a man of medium height, a handsome black Irishman, and there was a look of barely restrained fury in his tanned face. His right hand was in the pocket of his dark business suit and for a moment both Sam and John wondered with alarm if he had a gun in his pocket. The sight of the slight figure of the sheriff, who was leaving the courtroom now, was reassuring.

Bill Geary hauled up in front of the two lawyers and did not even glance at his ex-wife.

"You two barracudas ought to be happy, real happy!" His voice was trembling with anger.

"I should think we are," John Lillard said quietly. "We won for our client."

"You may have won for your client, but you've ruined me! Ruined me, you hear? Isn't once enough?"

"You had your chance to escape ruin before you even walked into that courtroom, Bill," Sam said.

"Why did she ask for that kind of alimony? Why should you two tell her to?" Bill raged at John Lillard.

"The judge thought you could afford it. So do I," John said curtly.

Bill Geary drew his hand from his pocket, and Sam, seeing what was coming, quickly stepped in between his father and Bill. The blow meant for John Lillard caught Sam flush on the nose. At Lola's scream, Frank Cosby, the sheriff, who was talking with Geary's attorney in the courtroom door, looked over.

Then he raced the few paces to Bill Geary. John Lillard had grabbed Geary's right arm, but Bill was slashing at Sam's face with his left fist. Sam had covered his face with his hands and blood was trickling from behind his palms. Frank Cosby lunged on Geary and succeeded in pinning his arms. "Quit it, Bill! Quit it!" he said sharply.

"Let me go!" Geary shouted. He directed a kick at John Lillard that missed by an inch, and then Cosby swung Geary around in a half-circle and shoved him against the wall, face against it. "All right, Bill, that's enough," the sheriff said. He loosed his hold on Geary and then stood between him and the two Lillards.

Cosby was a slight, red-haired, banty rooster of a young man dressed in Western boots, Oregon pants, checked shirt, and worn

Stetson; he had a .38 revolver strapped to his hip. There was a scar on his nose acquired in some long-forgotten brawl, and his blue eyes held both anger and toughness.

"What's got into you, Bill?" he demanded.

Bill Geary was panting from his struggle but he took a step forward, intending to brush the sheriff aside. The sheriff put a hand against Geary's chest.

"The next time I touch you it'll be on the head with my gun," Cosby said quietly. "It won't be exactly a touch either."

Geary regarded the group with a wild temper still in his eyes. Sam had his handkerchief to his nose and his eyes were still watering with the pain of the blow. Lola Geary's eyes were blazing with anger. Only John Lillard seemed unruffled, and now he said with a dryness in his voice, "He doesn't like the judge's decision, Frank."

"Why don't you toss me in jail?" Geary asked hotly of the sheriff. "I'll wind up there anyway for not paying alimony!"

"Take it easy," Cosby said softly. The sheriff turned his head to regard Sam. "Want to sign a complaint against Bill, Sam?"

Sam only shook his head.

"Both of them will have a chance to later, after I get through with them," Geary said angrily.

"That sounds like a threat," the sheriff observed.

Geary looked at him a long moment and then gave a huge and shuddering sigh. "Ah, the hell with it!" he said. He brushed past the sheriff and walked down the stairs that led from the second floor, and went on out to the street.

"If he feels so strongly about the decision, why doesn't he beat up Judge Overman?" John Lillard asked, and then smiled at his own mild joke.

"He likely wants to, but he'll cool off," the sheriff said.

"Not ever," Lola said flatly. "He's got the temper of a farrowing sow."

Frank Cosby grinned. "That's an expression I'd forgotten." He looked at Sam now. "Sam, do you want to wash up?"

Sam took the blood-soaked handkerchief from his nose, which was still bleeding, and looked at his blood-spattered shirtfront. "Thanks, Frank, but I'll go over to the office. I have a clean shirt there." He put the handkerchief back to his nose.

John Lillard stepped up to Lola Geary and said, "Goodby, my dear. I think I'd better get Sam over to the office."

"Thanks, both of you, for everything you've done."

11

John smiled. "You should thank the judge, but I don't think he'd appreciate that," he said. He nodded at the sheriff, then touched Sam's arm. Sam said good-bye and they went down the stairs and left the courthouse.

The red brick courthouse, with its marble figure of a Union soldier inside the enclosing wrought-iron fence, faced a small park on the edge of Ute City's modest business district. On the very edge of town, both in front of and behind the courthouse, spruce-clad mountains with their scattered patches of bare aspen vaulted up to ten thousand feet. They were scarred by old mine dumps. The town, much longer than it was wide, lay on the narrow floor of a high mountain valley, bisected by the Ute River, and its brick and stone business buildings dated from the days of the silver boom in the late 80's and early 90's.

The ground-floor offices of Lillard and Lillard across the park from the courthouse were in one of these tall-windowed, high-ceilinged brick structures. When Sam and John pushed open the door, they were in a large reception room, furnished with a Victorian sofa, table, and chairs. There was a fire in the room's fireplace, and seated behind a flat-topped Victorian desk was Jessica Morfitt, their secretary. She caught sight of Sam's bloody handkerchief and came to her feet, a look of controlled alarm in her face.

She was a small girl, dressed in a loose-fitting tweed suit that did not do her full figure justice. Her hair was black, as were her unplucked eyebrows; they gave her pale, gold-flecked grey eyes an almost animal alertness. Whatever hairdo was current or would be current, Jessica ignored. Her hair was parted on the left side, and its curling blackness did not quite reach her shoulders.

"Sam, what's happened?" she asked.

"Just a bloody nose," Sam mumbled. He walked past her desk and opened the door in the back wall which led onto a short corridor. The first room to the right was a law library, beyond which, on either side of the corridor, were the Lillard's separate offices. The door at the end of the corridor opened into the lavatory, and Sam was already stripping off his coat and tie when he entered it. Jessica and John followed him.

Sam leaned over the washbowl and let the blood drip slowly from his nose.

"Give me a coin, Judge," Jessica said.

John Lillard, who had been a county judge for much of his adult life, reached in his pocket and handed her a dime. Swiftly, Jessica yanked a piece of tissue from its wall holder, wrapped the coin in it, thrust it in front of

Sam, and said, "Under your upper lip, Counselor. Press hard."

Docilely, Sam obeyed. When he straightened up, Jessica saw the cut on his broad nose.

"That door fought back, it looks like," she observed dryly. Reaching beyond him, she opened the medicine cabinet and brought out a box holding strips of adhesive tape. With another piece of tissue, she sponged the cut and applied the tape. Backing away to survey her handiwork, she then shuttled her glance to the Judge, who was watching.

"I've heard of courtroom fights, Judge, but I thought they were only a figure of speech."

"Bill Geary didn't like Judge Overman's orders. He took on Sam and was starting on me when Frank rode him down."

"In the courtroom?"

"Just outside," John Lillard said.

"But why you and Sam, Judge?"

"Lola was awarded the house and a thousand dollars a month alimony."

"Wow!" Jessica exclaimed. "Well, Bill had to hit somebody after that."

The Judge smiled faintly. "You should always ask for more than you hope to get, but this time we got what we asked for."

"Why isn't Bill mad at Judge Overman?"

John Lillard said dryly, "You don't beat up

14

district-court judges. Only ex-county
I guess."

"Not county judges, junior partne͟ ͟,
said wryly.

He pushed past Jessica into the corridor
and opened the door opposite the Judge's. Jessica, a frown of puzzlement on her face, followed the Judge into his own office. She
halted in front of the big desk while the Judge
seated himself in the leather chair behind it.

"This doesn't seem possible," Jessica said.
"Why was Bill mad at you two? You're only
Lola's attorneys."

The Judge sighed. "It was me he was mad
at, Jessie. It goes back a few years. I was
chairman of the loan board at your father's
bank. Bill Geary applied for quite a sizable
loan to start up in the insurance business." He
added, "You don't remember what Bill Geary
was when he was younger."

"I've heard."

"Well, your dad believed in making character loans. Bill Geary in those days didn't have
any character whatsoever. He was a drunk and
a woman-chaser — almost everything unattractive in a man." The Judge spread his
hands. "I turned down his request for a loan
for what I thought was good reason. He's
never forgiven me. On top of that, today's
business was just too much."

'Wasn't Judge Overman a little rough, udge?"

The Judge shrugged his heavy shoulders. "Maybe. Still, once everybody has cooled off maybe we can persuade Lola to accept less alimony."

"That means you think Bill Geary got a rough deal," Jessica observed dryly.

The Judge closed his eyes, leaned back in his chair, and rubbed his eyelids with thumb and forefinger. Then his hand dropped to his lap. "Yes, a little rough," he conceded. "Still, Bill was evasive and uncooperative, and I think Judge Overman was sore about Bill's attitude. I think the judge extracted more than the customary pound of flesh in this case."

"But Lola's family has money and they're generous with it, I've heard."

The Judge nodded. "She'll be in tomorrow." At that moment Sam entered the room, tucking the tail of a clean shirt under his belt. His father looked at him and smiled faintly. "I think Sam can start softening up Lola. After all, it was our idea to ask for what we did. Maybe Sam can persuade her that we asked for too much."

Sam gingerly fingered his nose bandage, his blue eyes holding a look of irony. "I'm not sure I want to. Besides, you're the sage advisor in this firm."

The Judge protested with mock sincerity. "Why, Sam, you know I'd talk to Lola but I won't be here tomorrow."

"I know," Sam said. "Instead of doing your duty, you and Hutch Cameron will be heading for the high country on a hunting trip. I'm supposed to clean up all the office grief while you're shooting at an elk. I said shooting *at* them. You'll notice I didn't say killing them."

The Judge grinned. "I'll remind you of that remark when you eat your first elk steak."

Mrs. Johnson, the Lillard's housekeeper, was cleaning off the dinner table in the dining room of the big mansard-roofed house that evening when the doorbell rang. She was closer to it than either of the Lillards, so she moved into the hall with a slowness that age and her Percheron weight made mandatory.

She opened the door to see Lee McPhail teetering on the edge of the porch, his face lifted to regard the night's weather. At the sound of the door opening, he turned — a tall man in his early thirties in the green jacket and Stetson hat of a warden of the State Game and Fish Commission. McPhail wore cowboy boots that raised his towering six foot one a couple more inches.

"Hello, Mac. You'll be after the Judge, so come in," Mrs. Johnson said.

Mac nodded and smiled as he swept off his hat. He was a lean man with a long, weather-browned face; his close-cut hair was only a shade darker. His eyes were so black they seemed pupilless; his ears were large and faintly bat-winged, which, added to the deep creases that made a parenthesis centered by his wide mouth, gave him something of the appearance of a friendly hound.

"Evening, Mrs. Johnson. I suppose the Judge is loading his musket," Mac said as he stepped into the hall.

"He's too old to hunt and he knows it, but try to tell him."

"You're never too old to hunt till you can't hold up a gun, Mrs. Johnson."

"They're in the library," Mrs. Johnson said. She turned back into the dining room and Mac moved into the living room, which was furnished with fine Victorian furniture of the kind whose overflow furnished the Lillard's law office.

Through the door into the library, Mac could see the stocky body of Sam Lillard seated in an easy chair. He was wearing a beat-up smoking jacket that was his uniform in the house. Sam, Mac thought, was almost a cartoon of a sedentary lawyer — physically lazy, somewhat overweight, slow-moving, pallid-faced, and brilliant. Upon his graduation *summa cum laude* from Harvard Law School, he had rejected all offers from big-city law firms, to return to Ute City, where he ignored the mountains, the streams, the hunting, the fishing, and the skiing. His only exercise, Mac knew, was playing billiards with his father on the table in the basement. Mac halted now in the doorway of the library.

Sam Lillard was talking. John sat on the leather sofa that was backed against a solid wall of books. The Judge, who in anticipation of tomorrow, was already wearing his red flannel shirt, had the bolt out of his Model 70, and was cleaning his gun.

Mac, who moved as noiselessly as a stalking animal, had not been heard. Now he said, "You'd better straighten that barrel, Judge." The Judge looked up and Sam turned his head.

"Well, I wondered when you'd be around," the Judge said cordially.

"He hasn't missed touting you on to game since he was a kid, Dad," Sam said.

"Naturally. I bribe him with the deer and elk tongues," the Judge said. "Sit down, you pensioned-off basketball player."

Mac grinned and moved over to the straight chair in front of the desk. He straddled it, unzipped his Eisenhower-type jacket with the Game and Fish patch on the shoulder, and

19

folded his arms on the top of the chair's back.

"You and Hutch got your spot picked, Judge?"

"You know better than that. We wait for you to tell us where the game is."

"You know those flat tops between Officer's Creek and Dry Woody?" Mac asked. "I flew over the place in the Department plane this afternoon. There's a big herd of elk up there, the biggest herd I've seen in years. There must be a hundred."

The Judge's shaggy eyebrows lifted in surprise. "Holy Moses, Mac! That country is way out in the back of nowhere." He gave Mac a mock tough stare. "I'm assuming that I'm the only one who has this information."

Mac laughed soundlessly. "You know better than that, Judge. We want that herd thinned out, so I've told a lot of people."

John Lillard snorted. "Big deal. Everybody in the whole damn country will be heading there tomorrow."

"That doesn't guarantee them an elk," Mac said. He turned to Sam and said teasingly, "You going with the Judge, Sam?"

Sam shook his head. "Somebody's got to keep the store." Then he said wryly, "Besides, if I did hunt, I think I lost so much blood today that I couldn't drag my carcass around."

"I heard about that," Mac said. "Bill always had a pretty low boiling point."

"I wish he had my nose right now," Sam said. "It's no use to me."

Mac got up and swung a leg over the chair. "Do you want a map, Judge?"

"I sure do," the Judge said emphatically. "That's a big country." He put down his rifle, moved over to the desk, and pulled out paper and pencil.

Mac took up the pencil and talked as he drew. "There are two or three roads into it, but I think the one through Mrs. Horn's ranch is the closest. You can short-cut a little by going through the corner gate in the north pasture. Here's where the herd is. They'll drop over the rim to water, then bed down in this area."

The Judge stood beside him studying the map. "What about this road, Mac?" he asked, and pointed.

"The hunters from Jamestown will probably use that one."

The Judge said ruefully, "It sounds as if you've spread the word all over the confounded state."

"Just half of it," Mac said, and then he grinned. "No, seriously, Judge, not too many cow elk permits were drawn around here. Of course, a lot of hunters from outside who've drawn permits won't know about this herd. Others have their favorite spots. I really don't think you'll have to take a traffic cop with you."

The Judge folded the map. "I hope you're right, Mac. Many thanks. Got time for a cup of coffee?"

Mac shook his head. "Thanks, anyway, Judge. I was due at Jessie's twenty minutes ago."

"When do you two get hitched, Mac?" Sam asked.

"Around Christmas, Jessie says."

"What's your family plan?" When Mac looked puzzled Sam said, "What I mean is — to put it indelicately — how soon can we expect Jessie to be pregnant?"

"Right after we're married," Mac said promptly.

Sam sighed. "Well, we'd better start looking for a new secretary, Dad."

"We'll look for two of them," the Judge said. "It'll take two to do Jessie's work." He sighed, "Well, I guess life has to go on, but why does it have to go on at the expense of Lillard and Lillard?"

Mac laughed and said, "Well, good hunting, Judge. Good night to you both."

After the day Lola Geary filed for a divorce,

Bill Geary moved out of their home and into a small apartment. It was close to his insurance agency, and he was surprised how undemanding apartment life was. There were no dogs to let in and out, no lawn to mow or leaves to rake, and no yammering television. On the other hand, his bed was empty and he was lonesome as hell.

Like Judge Lillard and like a hundred other able-bodied males in Ute City this evening, Bill was checking his hunting gear and clothes. His boots needed waterproofing, which was always a messy job. Moving into his bedroom, he stripped out of his white shirt and business suit, donned a T-shirt and a pair of levis, and returned to the living room. Clearing the coffee table of its cigarette box and ash tray, he spread out the morning newspaper to protect the table top, then went into the tiny kitchen where the waterproofing solution was stored in a kitchen cabinet. Before he returned to the living room, he rummaged around in the hall closet and found his boots.

He seated himself on the sofa and had just started to rub the waterproofing into his boots when the buzzer sounded.

"Come in!" he yelled. He heard the door open, and a second later Mac stepped into the room.

"Well, if it isn't the old beaver trapper,"

Bill said. "How are you, Mac?"

"Busy," Mac said.

"Doing what?" Bill asked skeptically, then added, "Want a drink?"

"Haven't got time for it, Bill. I thought I'd tell you about some elk I flew over today."

"Boy, will I listen!" Bill said.

Mac told Bill substantially what he had told the Judge earlier, but since Bill seemed to know the country, he did not bother with a map.

When Mac was finished, Bill said, "Man, I needed some good news today, after what I've been through. Did you hear about it?"

"I heard you went after Judge Lillard," Mac said. Then he asked quietly, "What the hell got into you, Bill?"

"Come to scold me?"

"What good would it do?" Mac asked wryly.

Bill picked up a cloth and started to wipe his hands. "In all the time I've known you, Mac, we've never discussed the Judge, have we?"

"I guess we both avoided it."

"I know he's a good friend and you're my good friend, but I can't abide the old boy."

"I suppose we all like two people who hate each other."

"Remember the loan he turned down, Mac?"

"I remember. I also remember you were the damnedest bum in town."

"Well, I made good in the business, didn't I?" Bill demanded.

"But all he had to go on was your past performance, Bill."

Bill shook his head. "All I know is that when I have anything to do with Judge Lillard I get dumped, like today."

"If anybody dumped you it was Judge Overman, not Lillard."

"Who do you think set that alimony price if it wasn't Judge Lillard?" Bill asked bitterly. "Hell, this goes back to the days of slavery. I work for Lola and she leaves me just enough for a roof and food." He added sourly, "Judge Lillard must have read the Hollywood papers to come up with a figure like that."

"Lola might get married again."

Bill said wryly, "I'd marry her again to get out of this."

At that moment the buzzer rang and Bill yelled "Come in!"

The door opened and George Maxwell stepped into the room.

"Hello, Mac. Hi ya, Bill."

George was an auto dealer and Geary's long-time hunting companion, a pudgy extrovert of Bill's age. He wore rimless glasses, a tidy business suit, a checkered top coat, and a hat that was too narrow-brimmed for his full face. It even had a red feather in its band. When George saw what Bill was doing, he said, "Damn, I've got to do that tonight too."

"I've got to run along, Bill. Good hunting, both of you," Mac said.

Both men said good-bye and Mac went out.

"How about mixing us a drink, George? I'm all gucked up."

George shucked out of his coat, threw it and his hat on the arm of the sofa, and headed for the kitchen. He said over his shoulder, "More whisky than water for you?"

"Like always."

Bill's hands were now covered with the waterproofing solution. His back started to itch and he leaned back against the sofa, rubbing against it. He wondered why it was that an itch always occurred when you were unable to scratch it. Presently George returned with the drinks, set both on the coffee table, then took off his suit coat, picked up his drink, and slacked into the easy chair.

After taking a sip of his drink, George said, "Old one-punch Geary. Boy, are you the talk of the town!"

Bill didn't even look up from his work as he answered, "I'd have gotten the Judge, too, if it hadn't been for Cosby." He paused and then looked stonily at George.

"You hear what they did in the court-room?"

"I heard. Brother, you better give up the insurance business and start robbing banks."

Bill's voice was tight with anger as he said, "I can't pay it, George! I just can't pay that much!"

"I know *I* couldn't."

"A court of justice!" Bill said bitterly. "Overman should be reprimanded, and the Lillards should be disbarred." His fists clenched. "Every time I think of it, I get so mad I'm sick, George."

"It's rough, all right. Can you appeal it?"

"I don't know," Bill said angrily. "I didn't even talk with Clyde. I just went out and walked for two hours, trying to make sense out of what had happened." He reached out for his drink and took half of it in two gulps. "It isn't as if we had kids. Lord knows I'd support them, but oh no, Lola didn't want kids."

"She's got money of her own, hasn't she, Bill?"

"Hell, yes! Her grandmother left her a bundle. She doesn't need the house and she doesn't need half the alimony that was granted. She doesn't need *any* alimony."

"Well, I guess even a judge can be influenced by a pretty girl."

"You don't have to guess. You know it now."

George pulled at his drink and looked as if he wanted to ask a question, and then thought better of it. Then he changed his mind. "Bill, it's none of my business, but what was it between you and Lola?"

"Everything," Bill said sourly. "I couldn't do anything that pleased her. I didn't make enough money, I drank too much, I didn't like her folks, I didn't take her out enough, and I had a terrible temper. All this *she* claimed. Well, I guess she was right about the temper, but not about the rest of it." He shook his head. "When it got to the point where I didn't want to go home, and didn't, she filed."

George shook his head. "You've given a short history of marriage, my boy, except that where love is involved, none of the other stuff really matters."

"There *was* love involved at first, but only on my part," Bill said.

The conversation had taken an embarrassing turn and George realized now that he should never have brought up the subject of divorce in the first place. He said now, "What I really came for, Bill, is to tell you we'd be crazy if we hunted Thrasher Park tomorrow."

Bill said, "I know. Mac told me about the

herd he spotted. Can we get a jeep in there?"

"I can get a jeep anywhere," George said immodestly. "Remember, I've got a winch in my jeep."

"Well, we've got a healthy day ahead of us, George, so make us another unhealthy drink."

Mac climbed into his green pick-up with its tall aerial and with the seal of the State Game and Fish Department on its doors. He switched on the radio to the channel shared by the Game and Fish Department, City Police, County Sheriff's Office, and the State Highway Patrol. Right now the City Police Department was chatting with the State Police regarding a break-in. Mac snapped off the radio, since by far the bulk of his communications, both receiving and sending, was done in the daytime.

Heading for Jessie's house, his thoughts returned to his talk with Bill. Somehow during the past five years he had contrived to keep the friendship of both Judge Lillard and Bill. Each of these men understood that Mac liked both of them and that any discussion of the other was off limits. Mac had taught Bill to hunt and to fish, and Bill had taught him to play a hard-headed game of poker. It was strictly a male companionship, since Jessie disliked Bill and Mac came close to disliking Lola.

In spite of his rough temper and his quiet dislike of the Lillards, Bill had a quality of warmth and generosity Mac admired. Bill had changed from a talented hell-raiser into a solid businessman, but he had retained that same charm and blarney that had made people of the town secretly like him even while they clucked disapproval. While Lola had found herself unable or unwilling to live with this stormy and mercurial man, it would seem, Mac thought, that the terms of the divorce settlement were extremely harsh.

Mac pulled up in front of the Morfitts' modest new home on the outskirts of a new development on Ute City's fringe. When Abel Morfitt, Jessie's father, was alive, the Morfitts lived in one of the big old-fashioned houses on one of the old elm-lined streets of Ute City. Abel had headed Ute City's National Bank before his heart attack; after his death the old place was too big for the mother and daughter. Besides, the house held too many poignant memories for both of them. With the money from its sale, they had built this one-story redwood-sided house that blessedly could never hold the associations of the other one.

As he went up the walk, Mac could see

Jessie and Mrs. Morfitt through the living-room window. Jessie was reading and Mrs. Morfitt was knitting. He punched the bell and stepped into the room as Jessie rose to answer the door. She was wearing black slacks and a fiery orange blouse that Mac had never seen before, and for a quick moment he regarded her with what she knew was admiration.

"Been spending your money, haven't you?" he asked. Then he added, "Evening, Mrs. Morfitt. Your daughter is dressed to catch a man."

Mrs. Morfitt was an older Jessie, and looking at her Mac hoped that his bride-to-be would age as gracefully as her mother. Mrs. Morfitt's black hair was streaked with grey, but her figure was as trim as a girl's. When she smiled at Mac, there was Jessie's warmth and quiet impudence in it.

After putting her hand on Mac's neck and pulling him down to her level, Jessie kissed him and then backed off. "Kissing you is a problem for me," Jessie said. "Either you should get down on your knees, or I should get an orange crate to stand on."

"It's no problem for me," Mac said. He moved toward her and put his hands under her arms, hoisted her, and kissed her.

"Should I leave the room?" Mrs. Morfitt asked.

31

"If you stand up, I'll do the same to you," Mac said. He threw his hat on a chair, took Jessie's hand, guided her to the long sofa, and set her down beside him. "What's new in the Morfitt household?" he asked.

"Did you hear about Bill Geary and Sam?" Jessie asked.

"From everybody in town."

"It was stupid on Bill's part, but I can't say I blame him. I know we're not supposed to criticize Judge Overman, but I do think a thousand dollars a month alimony is pretty rough," Jessie said.

"If you ever pull that on me, I'll move to Canada."

Mrs. Morfitt said dryly, "She'll have to get married first, Mac, before she can divorce you."

"McPhail is willing," Mac said. "Just prod your daughter."

"Now wait a minute!" Jessie protested. "All three of us agreed on the date."

"I just pretended to agree," Mac said.

"You're a fibbing phony!" Jessie said hotly. "You're the one who said you had to be here during hunting season and then go to the Commission Meeting!"

Mac frowned in concentration. "I don't remember saying that."

Suddenly Jessie knew she was being teased

and she laughed.

Mrs. Morfitt asked, "Did you draw the checking-station chore this year, Mac?"

"No, we've cut down on the number of stations. I guess someone looked at a map and discovered there's only one highway through here. They're putting them only at highway junctions this year. Me, I'll just be a cop for a couple of weeks."

"More of a cop than always?" Jessie asked with intended malice.

Mac only grinned, then looked at his watch. "Want to learn how to shoot ducks?"

"I've done a lot of crazy things on dates, but shooting ducks isn't one of them," Jessie said tartly. "Are you feeling all right?"

"I promised the Scouts I'd show them a film on ducks tonight. By the time you've made a pot of coffee, I'll be back."

"I never thought I'd be competing with Scouts, but go ahead," Jessie said.

The Justice of the Peace Court in Ute City was held in the one-room council chamber, whose walls were plastered with maps of the city delineating water, power, and sewer lines. The court was presided over by Justice of the Peace Oscar Landsman and it met in the evening, as tonight, because Landsman, one of the town's druggists, was too busy making his living during the daylight hours to convene his court.

Oscar sat behind the long table and faced three rows of folding chairs. He was a pallid, bespectacled man in his middle thirties, whose owlish eyes held a dry amusement as he regarded the two defendants seated in the first row. In the second row and well away from the defendants sat the red-headed sheriff, Frank Cosby, beside his hulking deputy, Harve Wallis. These five were the only people in the rather large room.

Oscar gaveled the court to order, then pitched the gavel on the table.

"Well, Chuck, you're getting to be such an old hand here, you don't need a lawyer."

Chuck Daily smiled without amusement, revealing a partial set of rotted teeth. He was a man in his forties, slight of build, and his rather pinched face with its four-day growth of beard was a study in contrasts. His blue eyes were alert and intelligent, but held a kind of animal cunning. His nose was big and long and his slack mouth gave his whole face an expression of contemptuous meanness. Looking at him, Oscar reflected that in the wrong way Chuck Daily was a legend in Ute City. His shiftlessness was used as a point of comparison, since he worked at the lowest of low-pay jobs only when he needed eating or drinking money. The former was seldom, since he was a dedicated deer poacher. The latter need occurred more often, for he was a devotee of the cheapest wine that could be bought. Oscar remembered that Chuck had served short terms in the county jail and a fairly long one in the state prison for robbing a liquor store. Oscar himself had contributed a work sentence or two. Chuck pieced out his minuscule income by trapping and by selling fish caught illegally to the local restaurants at bargain prices.

Now Oscar looked at Chuck's neighbor. "It seems you've been a bad girl, Minnie."

Minnie Gerba was a raddled woman of forty-five, with a wreck of good looks, who was wearing a heavy sweater that had raveled holes at both elbows. Now she spoke up.

"Well, it was my window he threw the bottle through, Judge. I never complained."

Oscar smiled faintly and looked beyond.

"What's the charge, Sheriff?"

"Harve made the call, Oscar. Maybe he'd better tell it."

Harve Wallis slowly hoisted himself to his feet. He was black-haired and dark-complexioned, with blue eyes that seemed startlingly pale in that face. He was a big man in his early thirties, dressed in a tan shirt, tan Oregon pants, and cowman's boots. When he spoke, his voice was rasping and authoritarian, suggesting that in some past time he had worn sergeant's stripes.

"The charge is drunk and disorderly, and disturbing the peace. This was on Saturday night. They woke up that whole end of town with their brawling and cussing and screaming."

"And they are charged as indicated?"

The deputy nodded. "It sure took two to make that fight."

"Describe what happened, Harve."

In a matter-of-fact voice, the deputy recounted how a call had come to him from a riverbottom resident complaining that Chuck and Minnie were engaged in a drunken brawl in the hard-packed yard of Chuck Daily's mean shack. When he arrived at the scene, the deputy said, Minnie and Chuck were wrestling on the ground, Chuck trying unsuccessfully to wrench a heavy piece of stovewood from Minnie's hand. The fight had drawn a crowd of interested neighbors, who could tell him nothing of how or why the fight had started. He had arrested them and he had thrown them in the county jail to sober up. After giving this account, Harve sat down.

Now Oscar's glance held a veiled amusement and he said to Chuck, "Anything to add to that, Chuck?"

"No."

"You, Minnie?"

"I don't remember anything."

"Well, how do you plead, Chuck? Guilty or not guilty on the two charges? One of drunk and disorderly, the other of disturbing the peace."

"What if I plead not guilty?" Chuck asked.

"You are entitled to a jury trial."

Chuck thought about this, then asked. "What if I plead guilty?"

Oscar asked impersonally, "Can you pay a fifty-dollar fine, Chuck?"

"You know I can't," Chuck said sourly. "I'm broke."

"Borrow it?"

"If you'll loan it to me." Chuck's tone was one of irony.

"I hardly think that would be proper," Oscar said dryly. "If you can't pay the fine, this Court will sentence you to thirty days in jail. You'll probably be working on the city or county road crew, wherever help is needed. Or I could give you the maximum of both a fine and a jail sentence."

"But my back!" Chuck whined. "I can't do no heavy work, Judge. You know that."

Oscar grimaced. "I seem to remember that." He drummed his fingers on the table and regarded Chuck with a mixture of distaste and admiration. "What you are saying is that

37

since you can't pay your fine, you'll go to jail. There, you'd be willing to sweep out your cell but couldn't do heavier work. The county will feed you three times a day for thirty days while you'll mostly read comic books and sleep."

Chuck did not bother to answer, because he had made his unarguable point. It had worked before, and it just might work again. However, a little reinforcement of his argument would help. He was willing to provide it.

"It goes past that, Judge. A man can't help it if he's got a sprung back. Still, that's no reason to starve him."

Oscar's eyes opened a little and he glanced at the sheriff to see if the sheriff had heard what he had heard. He found a faint mocking smile on the sheriff's young face. To Chuck he said, "A thirty-day free load at county expense is starving you?"

Chuck shrugged. "Not that. It's the rest of the winter."

Oscar frowned. "Back up a little. What is it you're trying to say?"

Chuck shot a swift glance at Minnie, who was listening as if in a trance.

"It's like this, Judge," Chuck went on. "You put me in jail and I can't work off my fine, so I'm a county charge, ain't I?"

Oscar nodded.

38

"And you'll have kept me in jail through the hunting season, won't you?"

Oscar knew Chuck was right. He searched his mind for Chuck's line of reasoning for a hint of what was coming. Since he could not find it, he said, "I guess that's so."

Chuck pounced then, but it was a slow pounce couched in a whining, hurt voice that held a little contempt too. "I've already spent all the money I got on an elk license and a deer license. I'm counting on a bull elk and a big buck for my winter's meat. How am I going to get them if you got me in jail?"

"You got yourself in jail," Oscar snapped.

"Maybe I did," Chuck said, but he was persistent. "If I can't get no meat and can't do no heavy work to buy food, then I got to go on county relief through the winter, don't I?"

"You don't have to, but you probably will," Oscar said shortly. "What're you getting at?"

"Just this," Chuck said flatly. "Opening day of hunting season is day after tomorrow. Don't start my sentence till I got time to get my winter's meat in. That'll mean I won't be on welfare and won't cost the county so much."

Now that it was out, Oscar regarded Chuck with open admiration. Everything Chuck said held a certain twisted and blackmailing logic. True, once Chuck had served his sentence, he would immediately start poaching deer enough to feed him through two winters. But it was equally true that Lee McPhail would very likely catch him, Oscar would sentence him, Chuck would be unable to pay his fine, and the county would have him as a non-paying guest for a couple more months. Better to let Chuck off for a month's grace before feeding him for thirty days, than to insist that his sentence begin tomorrow and have him as a prisoner for a total of three months. He knew this was Chuck's sly reasoning and he wondered what was behind it. The only reason that occurred to him immediately was that Chuck welcomed the chance to hunt legally and possess legal game. Chuck was probably tired of the eternal watchfulness required in hunting illegal game, both in killing it and in hiding it.

This doesn't take a Solomon, Oscar thought. Money was money, especially in a small, high-country county, whose monthly expenditures were questioned to the penny by watchful taxpayers. It was better to grant Chuck's request for a month's hunting and pay out fifty dollars for food, than not to grant it and then pay out an almost certain hundred and fifty dollars for his upkeep upon almost certain re-arrest and conviction for poaching.

Oscar looked now at Frank Cosby and felt a

little foolish as he asked his question. "Suppose I give Chuck a chance at hunting, Frank? Any objections?"

"It would be cheaper," Frank conceded.

"All right, Chuck. I'm postponing sentence till you've had your chance to hunt. You'll report to the sheriff after hunting season. I said I was postponing, not suspending, your sentence. Is that clear?"

"Much obliged, Judge."

Now Oscar turned his attention to Minnie. "Minnie, you've heard the charges against you. D'you plead guilty or not guilty?"

"I don't plead nothing," Minnie said. "I don't remember nothing, but nothing."

Oscar felt quiet exasperation stir within him. She knew exactly what she had done and would refuse to pay a fine so the county could support her for a relatively pleasant month. In a way, it would be a pleasant sojourn for her. She would not have to chop her own wood, cook her own meals, and slave away at ironing for the matrons of the town, with which she earned the most meager of livings. *This is my night to play Santa Claus*, Oscar thought, and he cleared his throat. "Minnie, I believe you when you say you remember nothing. I suppose it was Chuck who got you drunk?"

"I don't have money for drink, Judge. Yes, it was him."

The simpering innocence on Minnie's face could not have fooled a half-bright child, Oscar thought.

"Everything went black, did it, Minnie?" Oscar asked, a heavy irony in his voice.

Minnie seized upon this eagerly. "How did you know, Judge? That's the way it was. I was sitting in Chuck's house and I woke up in jail."

Oscar sighed and reached for his gavel. "Minnie, I hope you can see what overdrinking — " He paused, feeling the futility of any reprimand he might give her. "Oh hell," he muttered under his breath, then said crisply, "Case dismissed."

Down on the riverbottom road, the poorest section in town, Chuck and Minnie lived in mean shacks set across from each other. There were few street lights here, and as they approached their houses they were bedeviled by barking dogs that Chuck systematically cursed into silence. Minnie halted in front of her dark house and Chuck slanted off toward his. He did not bother to bid her good night.

"Chuck," Minnie called. "There was some wine left."

Chuck halted. "I thought you was drunk. I know I was."

"Come on, Chuck, let's have a drink. We

ought to celebrate getting out."

"I got a lot to do," Chuck said dubiously.

"I'll help you."

Chuck's tone was sour as he said, "All right. Come on."

The days in the overheated jail made the night seem more chill than it really was and a drink would be welcome, Chuck thought.

He preceded Minnie into his one-room shack, wiped a match alight on the seat of his pants, and crossed over to the table. He lighted the kerosene lamp, which stood on it, then turned to regard the room to see what damage had been done before the fight moved outside. The room held a stove, a sink with a pump on it, a cot with a couple of dirty blankets wadded up on it, a wall calendar three years out of date, and some guns stacked in the corner below an orange crate nailed to the wall that held ammunition. Chuck's spare wardrobe hung from nails above the cot.

Now he noticed that the table was sticky with spilled wine, but there was a third of a gallon of muscatel left in the jug. It could not have been much of a fight in here, Chuck thought. About all he could remember was that he tried to kick Minnie out and she would not go.

Without bothering to rinse out the dregs-filled cups, Chuck poured out a cup of wine

43

for each of them, then shucked out of his filthy jacket. While Minnie seated herself and started to sip her wine, Chuck built up a fire in the stove. Then he turned to the table, drank down his wine, and refilled his cup. Minnie began to laugh soundlessly.

"What's funny?" Chuck asked.

"You and your sprung back. That's what's funny."

Chuck almost smiled. "Fellow I knew in jail put me on to that. They can call in a doctor and X-ray the hell out of you, but they can't prove you ain't got a sprung back."

Now Chuck walked across the room to where his three rifles were stacked, picked up one, reached in the orange crate for a bottle of cleaning solvent and rags, then, carrying the rifle, he crossed over to his cot and sat down.

The room was beginning to warm up and Minnie unbuttoned her sweater. "You going tomorrow, or opening day?" she asked.

She was helping herself to a second cup of the muscatel, and Chuck, as he unscrewed the cap of the solvent bottle, looked closely at her. All their arguments started with some innocent conversation such as this. Truth was, Chuck knew, Minnie had no tolerance for alcohol, and he felt a sudden disgust. Her hair had been peroxided so often and so relentlessly that it looked like an ill-made wig. Her rather childlike face with its blue eyes was ravaged by loneliness, drink, and quiet despair. After her miner husband's death from silicosis five years ago, she had lived alone in her mean shack across the road, earning her living by cleaning the homes of the town's younger matrons and by taking in ironing. Out of her loneliness, she was promiscuous at every opportunity afforded her, which lately was seldom.

Chuck felt a contempt for her that had nothing to do with morals. In his sight she was nothing, one of the people who should never have been born, a woman who would drudge out her days unwanted and unneeded. A man, Chuck reasoned, had independence and a few solid pleasures. This woman had nothing but a friendless old age to look forward to — which was exactly what she deserved. The only reason Chuck tolerated her and let her drink his wine was because out of her loneliness she would cook him several meals a week in return for his company.

"I'll go out tomorrow, get the camp set up, and some wood chopped," he said.

"Where you going?"

"I heard from the sheriff a big herd of elk was spotted on the flat tops above Officer's Creek. I'll get one of them."

Minnie looked at the gun and then said on impulse, "Take me with you, Chuck. I can shoot a rifle, and you got two."

Chuck looked at her with contempt. To an extreme degree Chuck was a loner; he fished, hunted, and trapped by himself, and when he had to work or play with other men he was taciturn and sour.

"The two-seventy's busted," Chuck lied. "Besides, remember the time I took you fishing? I never heard so much damn yakking in my life. You'd chase game out of the whole country."

"I could stay in camp and cook."

"I can cook better'n you any day. No dice, Minnie."

"Ah, well, it was worth trying," Minnie said resignedly. "Just the same, I used to hunt with my husband."

"I bet he gagged you."

"He was a better hunter than you. He used to load his own bullets, too."

"Always the sign of a lousy hunter," Chuck said. "If he could hit anything, a box of shells would have lasted him three years."

"That's a thirty-ought-six, ain't it?" Minnie asked.

"So what if it is?"

"Nothing," Minnie said defensively. "What you so sore about? I was just going to tell you

46

it's exactly like the gun my husband owned. I had to sell it."

Chuck put down his wipe rag and looked at her. "Have you said one damn thing tonight that's made sense?"

Minnie looked startled. "Why, I don't know. I was just talking."

"Take another belt of wine and go talk somewhere else," Chuck said brutally.

Minnie drained her cup before she said. "Well, if that's the way you feel — "

Chuck interrupted her in a harsh voice. "Look, I got to get to bed. I don't give a damn if your husband hunted. I don't give a damn if he had a thirty-ought-six like mine. I don't give a damn if you had to sell it."

Minnie stood up. "All right, sorehead," she said angrily. "I was going to offer to cook your breakfast, but you can go to hell!"

Minnie crossed the room and went into the night, slamming the door viciously behind her.

After the hearing, Sheriff Frank Cosby said good night to Harve, chatted with Oscar for a moment, agreeing with his reasons for postponing Chuck Daily's jail term, then stepped out into the chill October night and reluctantly turned toward what another person would call home. To him it was not a home, for he and his young wife Selena lived in a basement apartment in the courthouse. This was dictated by the necessity that at all times he must be close to the police radio, and guard and feed whatever prisoners were in his custody. It might have been more of a home if his marriage had turned out differently, he thought, but what was done was done.

Turning in at the side entrance to the courthouse basement, he halted before his own door and took a deep breath as if to brace himself. His tough young face was altered by a look of pained resignation as he opened the thick door. Immediately, the crash of a TV program assaulted his ears and he shook his head imperceptibly. Hanging his Stetson on the hall tree, he stepped into the living room, where Selena was seated in an easy chair, back to the door. Frank winced, as he did each time he entered this room. While he was a plain man in his likes, he knew the taste that had furnished this room, with its overstuffed furniture, sentimental pictures, fringed lampshades, and frivolous pillows, was atrocious.

Passing by Selena, he went to the TV set and turned it down to a sensible level, then wheeled to look at his wife. She was in her late twenties and some three years younger than Frank, but she wore the expression of a harridan of fifty as she looked at him. Her pale hair had not been combed since breakfast. In repose her rather puffy face might have been called attractive, but it was seldom in repose. Indignation, sulks, anger, and self-pity could flit across it as the shadow of clouds race across a prairie. Right now, the expression was one of indignation. She pulled close the open collar of her chenille lounging robe as if this were not her husband watching her but some total stranger who might possibly ravish her.

"It might as well be off as like that," she said.

"That's what I think, too," Frank replied, and promptly switched the set off.

"There aren't any prisoners in their cells to keep awake, like you always say I'm doing!"

"No, but there's the rest of the town," Frank said. "I think you've used up your ration of eight hours' watching that screen today."

Selena rose. "I'm going to bed," she said hotly.

"Go ahead. It's probably still warm."

Now the tears came. Frank sighed, walked over, and took her in his arms. At first she put her palms on his chest trying to shove him away, but Frank held her tightly and she stopped struggling. Since the tears were manufactured, she could turn them off as easily as

49

she could turn them on, so now, a little affection shown her, the cry was over.

"Oh, Frank," she said into his shoulder, "why do you have to be this way?"

"If I had a kid that had ate candy all day, I'd belt him. I won't belt you, but I'll turn that damned thing off."

Now it was a sulk. Selena disengaged herself, flounced over to the sofa, sat down, picked up a magazine, and pretended to read.

"Any calls for me?" Frank asked.

"One. I didn't know where you were and besides they said it wasn't important."

"Didn't know where I was?" Frank said. "You saw me take Chuck and Minnie to the JP court."

"Oh, I forgot."

"Some day you'll forget to tell me there was a call that the bank had been robbed and the cashier shot."

Self-pity came now. "Stop picking on me, Frank! I just can't take any more of this. Living in this damned dungeon and cooking for those slobs of prisoners. Why can't we live like other people do?"

"With two TV sets instead of one?" Frank asked wryly.

Now it was anger again. "Now I *am* going to bed." Selena rose and started to cross the room.

Midway across it, she halted and turned to look at Frank. "I didn't hear you lock up Chuck and Minnie."

"I didn't."

"Don't tell me they had money to pay a fine."

"Not that either."

A look of puzzlement came over Selena's full face. "What happened, then?"

Frank crossed over to the sofa and tiredly sat on its arm. "Oscar postponed Chuck's sentence. He'll start serving it after hunting season."

"Why, I never heard of anything like that," Selena said. "Why did he do that?"

Frank stifled a yawn before he answered. "So Chuck could get in his winter supply of meat. If he hadn't, Chuck'd be on county welfare the whole winter, or he'd be in jail again for hunting out of season."

Now petulance came into Selena's face. "Frank, that's awful, simply awful!"

"What's awful about it?" Frank asked curiously.

"You know I was counting on the prisoner feeding money to buy me a new winter coat. What about Minnie?"

"Case dismissed."

The petulance changed to a pout as Selena stood in the middle of the room, glaring at her

51

husband. Suddenly she asked, "What did you say about Chuck being jailed for illegal hunting?"

Frank sighed and answered patiently, "I said if Oscar hadn't postponed the sentence and if Chuck had served his sentence during hunting season, Chuck would wind up as a county charge or else he'd wind up in jail for poaching. Either way it'd cost the county money."

Selena's expression became calculating. "Is the fine for poaching a stiff one?"

"Yes."

"So Chuck couldn't pay it and he'd have to go to jail?"

Frank frowned. "What are you getting at?"

Selena parried his question with one of her own. "Chuck is still your prisoner, isn't he?"

"Technically."

Selena came toward him now and halted before him. "Then stand on your rights. Demand that Chuck serve his sentence now. Anyway, whoever heard of a sentence being postponed!"

Frank frowned. "Why should I do that?"

"Don't you see?" Selena asked impatiently. "You've already said if Chuck's jailed through hunting season, he'll poach. You could watch his place, catch him with the meat, and he'd be jailed. A dollar and a half a day for feeding

52

him on a long sentence, Frank, isn't peanuts."

Frank came to his feet and stared at her incredulously. "Are you suggesting I frame Chuck so you'll get money for feeding him?"

"You aren't framing him!" Selena said angrily. "You'd make it necessary for him to poach and then you'd catch him. Mac'd help you."

Frank's face drained of color and his eyes were bright with anger. He said quietly, "Good night, Selena," and turned and went into the kitchen. He drew a glass of water from the sink tap and found his hand was shaking so that he spilled water on his shirt front.

The very thought of Selena's suggestion made him a little sick. He wondered now at how little she knew him and he knew her. She was not only brainless but truly greedy, and this last facet of her character he had never seen until now.

He began to pace the small kitchen, thinking over and over again: *This will never last, never.* The marriage had started out wrong and continued wrong, and he bitterly reviewed its course in his mind.

It started with himself, he supposed. Turned out of an orphanage at sixteen, he had bummed the country. One night he was arrested on suspicion of rolling a drunken miner in Montana and he had been savagely beaten by the sheriff, denied counsel, and beaten again and again. He was finally released for lack of evidence and floated out of town. But he *had* rolled the drunk; he *was* guilty and he had probably deserved the beatings he took, but what stuck in young Frank Cosby's mind was that, guilty or not, no man should be subjected to the deprivation of his rights, to the denial of counsel, and to the savage beatings at the hands of the Law.

After his release, he not only promised himself to go straight and did, but he was determined to become a law officer. In a way, this was a negative resolution. There were sixty-one counties in this state and maybe sixty-one sheriffs as heartless and cruel as the one in that Montana county. If he could be elected sheriff, then there might by sixty cruel sheriffs left, but not sixty-one.

After a hitch in the Marines, he had drifted to Ute City and applied for the deputy sheriff's job. The next election he had beaten the incumbent. Since his election three years ago, he had been just with the guilty and the not guilty, for as a man who had sinned he understood the sinner's need for compassion and mercy. And he had been lonely.

Jessica Morfitt, too, had played a part in his

marriage. He had met her, fallen head over heels in love with her, and had courted her with grim determination to win her. Mac had been his rival for Jessie's affections and it had not been a very friendly rivalry. Pushed almost to desperation by the attentions of the two men, Jessie had made her choice. She had promised to marry Mac.

Don't blame her, blame yourself, Frank thought. The rest of the story was almost childish, he knew. Out of defiance and spite, and out of a wish to show Jessie that he did not need her and that there were other attractive girls in the world, he had married Selena Graham, the pretty daughter of a seedy rancher up the valley. Thinking of it now, it was plain that he had married a stranger. He had walked, eyes open, into a marriage with a vain, stupid, dim-brained vegetable that he would have to shape up into some image of a real woman, or leave her. Only he knew it would be impossible to do the first, and miserably unkind to do the second.

II

The next day the usually quiet Main Street of Ute City was a hum of activity. There were hunters in the stores buying supplies, shells, and liquor. There was a constant traffic of pick-ups, trucks, jeeps, and horse trailers heading for the mountains to make camp before opening day. In the traffic on this chill overcast morning were the Judge and Hutch Cameron in Hutch's big truck that carried their camping equipment as well as three horses. An hour later, Bill Geary and Charlie Maxwell in a metal-topped jeep passed the town limits heading north. Still later, Chuck Daily in a battered, topless wreck of a jeep left town. The only things they had in common were red shirts, jackets, caps, and an enormous sense of anticipation.

Eleven miles north of town all three hunting parties — at separate times — turned off the highway onto a gravel road that petered out into a dirt road as it climbed past the low-lying ranches, until it was finally in spruce timber.

On the edge of the timber was the last ranch. It was owned by Mrs. Horn, who, with only occasional help, raised just enough hay to feed a small herd of cattle. Beyond Mrs. Horn's big log house the road petered out to a trail that joined fire trails and old logging and mining roads.

It was at the Horn ranch that the Judge and his big companion, Hutch Cameron, visited with Mrs. Horn for a while, then unloaded their horses and saddled up. Bill Geary and George Maxwell passed the ranch while they were unloading, but neither man saw them. They were just finishing the diamond hitch on the pack horse when Chuck Daily's jeep rattled past. They waved and he waved.

The Judge and Hutch headed out to the north pasture, heading for the high country. Bill Geary and George Maxwell followed an old logging trail for another eight laborious miles before they chose their camp site. Chuck cut off the logging trail onto an old mine road, which after seven miles proved to be so full of windfalls that he pulled off and bushwhacked till he came to a high meadow. Halfway around the perimeter, he found water and made camp. In the middle of the night it began to rain.

Well before daylight Hutch Cameron rolled

out of his sleeping bag, pulled on his heavy socks and trousers, wiped a match alight, and lit the gas lantern inside the tent. Hutch was five years younger than the Judge, and when they stood beside each other he towered over the Judge. A lifetime of ranching had given him hands the size of a fielder's glove, had browned his long face, and had wrinkled his skin at the corner of his pale eyes, which now squinted against the sudden glare of the lamp. Under his aquiline nose was a full mustache that was more gray than black.

Now Hutch turned to the Judge, whose back was to the lamp, and gently nudged him. "Come on, Judge. There's no elk in that sleeping bag. Hear that rain?"

The Judge roused, sat up, and listened to the rain on the tent. Both men had slept in their long-handled underwear and they dressed quickly against the chill morning. Hutch took the dry kindling he had cut the night before, turned on his flashlight, opened the tent flap, then halted.

"Judge, where's the can of gas? I'll need it to get the fire going," he said over his shoulder.

The Judge rose and took a big can of lighter fluid from his duffel.

The Judge and Hutch had been hunting together for so many years that long ago they had divided their camp chores. Hutch loaded the fire with wood he had cut the afternoon before, then rounded up the hobbled horses with his flashlight and grained them. The Judge, meanwhile, was preparing breakfast on the portable gas stove inside the tent. The wood fire was mainly for warmth and for boiling water for coffee. The Judge whistled as he stirred up the batter for the pancakes. The rain, he was thinking, was good news if it was not too heavy. While it cut down visibility, it made it easier to approach the game. Too, if there was no wind, it let a man approach closer. If there was a wind, a man could hunt into it knowing the game could not scent him.

These were the days the Judge lived for through the year. He liked his law practice and eagerly accepted its heavy responsibilities. Yet, when he awakened yesterday morning, it was as if sleep had washed all memory of those responsibilities from his mind and had replaced them with a boy's anticipation of what was coming. While he liked to fish, and did, hunting was something entirely different. When a man was fishing, he was confined to a stream whose every pool and ripple he probably knew, but in hunting, especially a new country, there were new sights that gave a man what every man longed for — a sense of exploration. There was always a new ridge and a new canyon, and appreciation of them was heightened by a sense of expectancy.

The Judge listened to the fire crackling and heard the raindrops hiss as they hit the fire. He also heard Hutch gently cursing the horses as he grained them. Presently Hutch came into the tent, his red hunting coat spattered with raindrops. Because the usual hunting cap was an unfamiliar and uncomfortable object to Hutch, he had pinned a red bandana over the crown of his beaten-up Stetson.

"This could likely turn into snow later."

"Hope so, but these October storms never last long, Hutch. It'll likely taper off by noon." He added, "See if that coffee's boiling, will you?"

Hutch stepped out and returned with the big granite coffee pot as the Judge dished out the breakfast of pancakes, eggs, and sausage onto the two big granite plates.

Both men ate ravenously and in silence, and afterwards they both packed their pipes and lighted them.

"Let's have another look at your map, Judge," Hutch said. The Judge extracted Mac's map from his breast pocket and handed it to Hutch, who studied it in silence. Then he said, "I take it these circle things are open parks."

"That's right."

"So we head northwest."

The Judge said again, "That's right."

Hutch rose, then he stretched. "Lay them plates out in the rain and let nature do your washing. I'll make the sandwiches."

The Judge went out with the two plates and Hutch rummaged in the grub box, from which he extracted bread, cheese, and ham and made the sandwiches, which he put into a sack.

When the Judge returned he said, "Getting light."

"Well, let's saddle up."

By the time they had the two horses saddled, it was light and still raining. Hutch observed, "Reckon they'll be in the timber today."

Hutch hobbled the pack horse and turned him loose while the Judge brought their rifles from the tent and shoved them into the saddle scabbards. Afterward both men mounted, crossed the tiny stream, and headed north through the timber.

Three miles north of the Judge's camp, Chuck Daily was hunkered down on a log beside the campfire in the falling rain. Scorning a tent or an air mattress, Chuck had cut spruce boughs for a mattress and had spent the night comfortably in his sleeping bag under a thick spruce. After putting on his boots and building his fire, he had taken two quick belts from a quart of bourbon he had blown himself to. When he finished breakfast, he poured himself half a cup of coffee and filled it the rest of the way with whisky. Unaccustomed to the regular intake of whisky, Chuck found himself pleasantly drunk. He thought, regretfully, that it would not last, since he would walk it off.

Having finished his coffee royal, he went over to his sleeping bag and hung it on a spruce limb out of the rain. The carton containing his food he stored in the jeep, which he had parked back in the trees, and covered it with a dirty blanket that had sheltered his rifle from the rain. Picking up his 30.06, he checked his pockets for shells as he turned away from the jeep; then he halted and came back. He might as well have another drink, he thought, and thinking this, he took the bottle from the carton and took two deep drinks of the raw whisky. It jolted him like an electric shock and he stood there with his stomach churning, wondering if he was going to lose his breakfast. In a minute the nausea died and Chuck corked the bottle, covered the carton, and headed east out of his camp in the sleeting rain.

The Judge and Hutch had ridden less than an hour when the rain abruptly turned to snow. It was a hard, driving snow falling so fast and furiously that it seemed as if nature was going to unload a whole winter's snow in one day.

Hutch reined up and shouted above the wind at the Judge, "Ever seen anything like this?"

"Not this time of year."

"Can't see game in this," Hutch shouted.

"It's bound to slack off."

Hutch nodded and they both rode on. An hour later they picked up the tracks of a pair of elk in the snow on a ridge. The tracks went down a gentle, open slope to the north. Ahead of them they could see through the driving snow a park with a long and wide island of timber dividing it. They followed the tracks down almost to the spruce island when Hutch, who was in the lead, reined up. He let the Judge catch up with him, then pointed to the tracks in the three inches of snow.

"Figure that out, Judge."

The Judge looked down at the snow, then said, "They separated. Yeah," he added dryly, "he and his wife must have had a fight."

"Take your pick and we'll split up, Judge."

"You take the boy and I'll take the girl, Hutch. I've got a cow permit."

Hutch looked down the gentle slope, which was hidden by the snow. "Let's say we'll meet back here, Judge, in two hours. That suit you?"

"Agreed," the Judge said. He pulled his horse around. "Good luck, Hutch."

"If I get him I'll bet you could float an axe in the gravy he makes. Good luck, Judge."

They separated in the snowstorm.

Chuck's course after leaving camp that morning was slightly northeast and he was miles from it when the snow began. It was a sudden, wind-driven, heavy snow, and soon Chuck wished it would break so that he could get some idea of the lay of the country. Right now there was more than enough snow to track in. Even in a snowstorm and with close to a pint of whisky in his belly, Chuck's sense of direction was unerring.

One result of the whisky was that it was only when the snow was driving around him that Chuck remembered that he had not loaded his rifle. He remedied this quickly and tramped on, coming to an occasional small open park. He stayed close to the edges of the timber surrounding them, aware that the game would probably take shelter in the trees.

Presently he picked up some deer tracks which seemed fairly fresh. Although he was tempted to hunt the deer, he reflected that if he wasted time killing a buck and dressing it out, the chances were other hunters would find the elk herd before he did. It was really snowing hard and blowing hard now, and by the time he felt the ground gently sloping down to the north, several inches of snow had fallen.

Clinging to the edge of the timber, he could barely make out across the open stretch to his left the timber on the far side of the park whose fringe he was traveling. The visibility seemed to him to worsen. He was about to look away when he thought he caught a movement against the timber across the park. Halting, he cupped his hands on either side of his eyes to keep out the driving snow and tried to pick up the movement again. In a brief lull in the storm, he caught the movement again and tried to give it some shape through the wind-driven snow. Whatever it was, it was moving down hill.

The timber across the park seemed to end at the base of a hill in a jagged line of peninsulas and bays. Crossing one of these bays, Chuck now saw the four long legs of an elk in motion, briefly silhouetted against the snow.

He thought quickly. He himself was screened from the elk's sight by the timber. If he moved out to cross the park, he would spook the elk.

Kneeling now, he snapped off the safety of his rifle, raised his elbow on his knee, and tried over his sights to pick up the moving animal. He could make out only a vague shape. Then he saw that the elk would again cross another shallow bay and would again be silhouetted against the snow behind it.

He sighted on the bay and waited. Presently the four long legs came into dim sight, silhouetted against the snow as before. He could not see anything but legs, since the animal's upper body blended into the timber. But he had enough to go on. Icily calm, he carefully sighted, just behind the foreleg and above it, and squeezed the trigger.

He saw the animal go down and he felt a quiet elation. *That's some shooting, if I say so myself,* Chuck thought. He ejected the empty cartridge case into the snow and a fresh cartridge slipped into the chamber. Then he rose and headed for the downed animal, his pulse racing.

Slogging through the snow, he kept an eye on the animal, and as he drew closer he began to pick up a bit of color. It was red. *That's blood. My slug must have cut his throat,* Chuck thought. He took ten more steps through the driving snow and then as a squall of snow slacked off a bit so that he could see better, he halted. A cold apprehension arose in him.

That's no elk, he thought. Slowly and with mounting dread he moved closer, swinging a little way down the slope for a better view. What he thought was the bright blood of a dying animal turned out to be a red hunter's jacket half hidden by the downed animal, and the downed animal was a horse.

"Oh, Christ!" Chuck whispered. He came closer, almost on tiptoe, and now he could make out the leg of a man, the foot still in the stirrup. The strange angle of the leg told him that his bullet had shattered the leg before the slug went into the horse and killed him.

Chuck swung wide and he could hear the groans of the hunter, whose other leg was pinned under the horse.

And then taking another step, he saw through the driving snow the body and the face of Judge Lillard, who was looking at him.

Chuck Daily almost fainted then with pure terror. For a few agonizing seconds of thought he knew what lay ahead of him. With his notorious record it would surely be jail and a heavy fine.

Now Judge Lillard's voice, muffled with pain and by the snow, came to him.

"Chuck, you drunken bastard!"

The anger and contempt in those four words told Chuck what he could expect.

I should never have come close, Chuck thought

in panic. *Now he knows who shot him.* He watched as the Judge's head sagged, and he knew the Judge had fainted. Chuck's mind at last began to function.

Half of his mind said, *Nobody saw me except the Judge. Any hunter could have shot him. Who'll know it was me?* The other half of his mind answered, *The Judge knows it's you.*

Then Chuck Daily, the loner, made the loneliest decision of his life. He raised his gun, took careful aim at Judge Lillard's chest, and squeezed the trigger. The Judge's body was jolted and then he lay still.

Now real panic came to Chuck and he thought, *I've got to get out of here now. I've got to lose myself in this storm.* He started down the slope at a trot and then suddenly halted. When they found the Judge and saw that this was murder, they would search exhaustively for any clue the killer left. And he had left a clue: the ejected cartridge case from his first shot.

He turned and went back, picked up his tracks crossing the park, and found where he had knelt to shoot. Nearby was a slot in the snow where the hot cartridge case had melted its way below the snow's surface. Chuck reached down, found the case, then rose and headed down the slope, keeping to the edge of the timber.

Now that the deed was done, Chuck's sanity was returning. He had one cartridge case and the other empty one was in his gun, so there were none of his fingerprints available. He had the only evidence that could convict him. The thing to do now was to get out of the area.

As he tramped through the snow, he knew that if the Judge's body was discovered soon, its finder would try to track him. That was simple enough, for even if the snow drifted his tracks, they could still be followed. They would leave a shallow depression, no matter how much it snowed. The thing to do then, was to find other tracks and mingle his own with them so that tracking him successfully would be impossible.

From past years of hunting, Chuck knew that no matter how big the hunting area, a man always ran across the sign of other hunters. Chuck had walked only half an hour when he heard the sound of distant shots off to his left. Immediately he turned into the spruce timber and headed in the direction of the shots.

Within twenty minutes of walking, he came across what he was looking for. He found the tracks of three hunters who had apparently traveled single file through the thick timber of the ridge. Chuck followed in their tracks for half an hour, then unerringly headed back to his camp and his jeep.

He sought the bottle of whisky at once and took two deep drinks. Then he got his fire going and huddled down beside it, his hands held out against the fire for warmth. Carefully he now reviewed everything that had happened. He was certain that he had covered his tracks and that it would be a hopeless job for anyone to sort out his tracks among the others. By the time the Judge was found Chuck's tracks would be deeply drifted. And the body would be found, he knew, because when he passed the Judge at the Horn ranch, Hutch Cameron was with him. Hutch would search when the Judge did not show up. If Chuck fled the country now his actions would be highly suspicious, since Hutch knew he was here.

No, he must stay here as if nothing had happened. There was only one thing wrong with that, Chuck realized gloomily. The sheriff or one of his deputies would dig out the slug from the horse's body or from the Judge's body, ask for the guns of the known hunters in that area, and have the FBI Lab run a ballistics test. Chuck knew this procedure from the gun magazines and outdoor magazines that he read. For now this was not a hunting accident — it was murder, Chuck knew bitterly. Right now his panicky shooting of the Judge seemed foolish and insane, but a man had to act at a given time with the best judgment he could muster. His judgment, he knew now, had been bad, all bad.

Oddly enough, he felt no guilt just as he had never felt guilt for any of his actions. What he felt now was the purest kind of fear — fear of discovery, and his mind returned again to the problem of the inevitability of a ballistics test and the demand by the law that he submit his gun to one.

Taking another drink from his bottle, Chuck wondered again: *Shall I run for it and bury the gun?* And again he was sure that running would be the admission of guilt that would trap him.

And then an idea began to take shape in Chuck's cunning mind. If he could substitute another gun for his own 30.06, then the ballistics test would clear him. He had his own 270 at home, but home was a three-hour drive.

He began to reason closely. If the Judge's body was discovered soon, the first act of the man who discovered it would be to report it and get the body out. This would take time. Why, then, could he not leave right now for town, hide the 30.06, and return with the 270? With this plan settled in his mind, Chuck rose, brushed the snow from his jacket, and stamped out his fire. Then he took his bed roll to the jeep, and started back in low, low gear for the mine road.

As he drove he knew that the tracks he was making now would indicate to anyone investigating later that he had left camp and returned. What was his story to be?

Why, that's easy, Chuck thought immediately. He had shot a buck which, along with the elk he was certain to get, would be too much of a load for his jeep. His story would be that he had taken the buck back to town and returned. Undoubtedly they would ask him to prove he had a buck hanging at home.

Chuck smiled into the storm. That would not be hard.

Hutch Cameron tracked his bull elk for half an hour, then, judging that he was closing in, he dismounted and made the classic still-hunt circle downwind to get ahead of his quarry. However, Hutch had no luck, for when he came upon the bull's tracks at last, he saw where the bull had stood, then turned at right angles uphill through the timber at a run. Hutch knew what had happened. The shifting wind of this storm had undoubtedly carried his scent to the elk. On a less windy day he would have had his bull.

Tramping back to his horse, he wondered

how the Judge had made out. He had heard a couple of distant shots off to the south which could be from the Judge or it could be from another hunter. This area would surely be full of them today.

Hutch's still-hunt took time, and when he reached his horse he mounted and looked at his watch. He saw that he was going to be late for the rendezvous at the place where he had left the Judge. When he reached it the Judge was not in sight, and since he had lost his own elk, he figured that he might as well join the Judge, help him skin out his meat if he had got any, and if he had not, hunt on together with him. The tracks of the Judge's horse, though drifted over, were easy to follow. The Judge had kept to the edge of the timber as he rode down the long slope. Hutch hoped the Judge would be in luck this morning. The first day of the season a man's chances were best. After opening day the game would be scared, wary, and more difficult to locate and shoot.

Hutch roused himself to find that his horse had slowed its pace and its ears were pointed forward. He kicked the big sorrel in the flanks, but instead of moving faster the horse halted, ears up. Then he stood uneasily, and Hutch peered ahead into the storm but could see nothing. A bear? Hutch wondered. Or maybe a bobcat or a mountain lion. Certainly, with all the promised hunters in this country, the placid routine of its wild life would be disturbed.

Hutch moved into the timber, dismounted, and prudently tied the reins of the sorrel to a branch of a spruce. Then he moved back into the open park and tramped on down the hill, his rifle at the ready.

He had walked less than fifty yards when he caught sight of a big dark object lying in the snow. Puzzled, he moved forward. When he came closer and saw the red color alongside the dark form, he began to run, feeling a premonition that was almost unbearable. When he came closer he saw the Judge's smashed leg kited awkwardly over the side of his horse.

"Judge!" Hutch shouted.

There was no answer, and as Hutch skirted the horse he saw the shattered leg where blood had seeped through the pants. He felt a surge of relief. Some hunter had shot the Judge's horse, which had fallen on him. The Judge had probably fainted from loss of blood. Swiftly circling the horse, Hutch now saw that the Judge lay on his back, his eyes closed, his body and face almost drifted over with snow.

Hutch knelt beside the Judge and shook his shoulder. The shoulder gave, but there was no reaction. Hutch took off his glove and felt the Judge's cheek. It was cold, and a black dread came to Hutch. Swiftly he unbuttoned the Judge's coat and shirt and put in his hand to feel for his heart. His hand came away sticky, and now Hutch looked at his big hand that was covered with the Judge's blood. Stupefaction held him motionless. Then he ripped open the Judge's shirt and underwear and saw the death wound.

"No! No!" Hutch shouted, and did not know he spoke. For a stunned two minutes he knelt there, a nameless grief blotting out all thought.

Then slowly the full realization of what he saw before him came to him. The shot that broke the Judge's leg and killed the horse could not have hit the Judge in the chest. There had to be a second shot.

The Judge had been murdered, then!

A cold rage overwhelmed Hutch. A man could shoot a horse by mistake in the snowstorm. If that happened, the normal thing for a hunter to do would be to come up to what he thought was the elk. He would discover his mistake, then do everything in his power to get the rider out from under the horse and staunch his wound. Instead, the hunter had seen what he had done, had probably lost his head, and had killed the Judge.

Why had he? The only sensible reason, if it

could be called sensible, was that the hunter knew he had been recognized.

Slowly Hutch rose. He started out in a series of ever-widening circles around the horse and the Judge, and on the third circle he came across the tracks of the killer.

Hutch dogged the drifted tracks across the park and saw where the killer suddenly turned downhill at the edge of the timber. When he came to a clear boot-print under a spruce tree, Hutch shucked off his coat, and covered the track. He did not know why he did this, but he thought perhaps an impression of the boot-print might be taken which would be of value tracking down the Judge's killer.

Now Hutch went back to his horse, mounted him, and tried to force him to approach the Judge's dead horse. The sorrel fought like a tiger. Hutch knew he would have to give up any thought of packing out the Judge's body on the sorrel. However, he did get the sorrel close enough that he could get his rope around the dead horse's neck and drag him far enough so that he could lift the Judge out and lay him straight in the snow. By now Hutch was crying.

Almost blindly he mounted his horse and headed back toward the camp. He knew that their pack horse, used to the smell of blood on hunting trips where he packed out the game, would accept the burden of the Judge's shattered body.

Opening day of the hunting season found Mac in the Game and Fish pick-up making the spot checks that were his assignment. Cruising the back roads that were slick with the snow, he would stop when he saw a parked car if there were hunters in or around it. If they already had game, he checked to see if the game was tagged; and if it was not tagged yet, he would make a friendly suggestion to the hunters that they better tag up before they started to travel. If they had no game and were starting out, he would make suggestions as to good hunting areas. Always he would ask to see a license.

All that morning and afternoon his pick-up radio was on and he listened to the exchange of messages between the sheriff's office and State Police headquarters. Bob Canaday, the warden of Jamestown, reported that a hunter had broken his leg in a fall and was on his way into Ute City. Would they notify Doc Kimball to be ready for him? There was a bad accident resulting from the slick conditions of the roads on the other side of Ute City, the state patrolman reported. He would need an ambulance. And so it went. Mac reflected that it

77

was mostly misery or trouble that came over this common channel.

And then Mac was yanked alert as his number was called. He braked to a halt on the slippery road and listened closely.

"77 calling 110, 77 calling 110, come in and report your location."

Mac lifted the transmitter off its hook, pressed the button, and spoke into it. "110 to 77. I am eighteen miles northwest of Ute City on the Union Reservoir Road."

The sheriff's unpleasant voice came back at him. "77 to 110. Come to the Horn ranch on the Officer's Creek Road, Mac. Judge Lillard has been killed in a hunting accident. I'll meet you there. K3208."

Mac sat utterly motionless and stunned, unable to accept the enormity of the news. It took minutes for his mind to comprehend and accept the fact that the Judge would no longer fish or hunt or yarn with him any more. *Poor Sam, poor Jessie*, he thought, and his throat ached with the effort to check his tears. He was not wholly successful, and he wiped his eyes with his sleeve.

He turned the pick-up around on the narrow road and headed back to the highway. He had forty-odd miles to go before he reached the Horn ranch, and the last part of it would be tough traveling. As he drove, he wondered how the accident had happened. The Judge knew guns and respected them. He could not have shot himself accidentally. Then, too, there was no more careful man with a gun in the country than Hutch Cameron. Neither of them could have been responsible for this appalling happening.

Mac turned the yammering radio lower till he could hear the steady click, click of his windshield wipers. A sudden skid reminded him he was in two-wheel drive and he shifted into four-wheel, paying more attention to his driving.

Inevitably, though, his mind returned to the Judge. He remembered many of the wonderful generous acts of the man, especially for himself. The McPhails had been anything but a rich family; Mac's father had been a railroader and they lived in Granite Junction, a division point. When Mac was ten his father was killed in a railroad accident, and because his mother had a sister in Ute City they had moved there. To help out the meager income of the two women, Mac worked after school hours as a printer's devil. His weekends, however, were his own and from dawn of Saturday morning until after dark of Sunday evening, Mac hiked and hunted these mountains he loved and fished its streams.

It was almost at the headwaters of the Ute

River that he first met Judge Lillard, then in his forties. He had come upon Judge Lillard fishing and, without the Judge knowing it, Mac had watched him for a long time. He was witnessing something that first puzzled and then delighted him. The Judge, in breast waders, was fishing upstream with a dry fly that floated back to him after each cast. He took many fish and gently turned them back, keeping only an occasional one. Mac, whose idea of fishing was to dangle worms or salmon eggs in a deep pool, had never seen anything like this.

Presently, when the Judge waded out of the river to smoke a pipe, Mac revealed himself. He asked the Judge what this kind of fishing was called and the Judge explained the art of dry-fly fishing to him. He demonstrated the proper cast and float, then gave his rod to Mac and coached him for half an hour. It was close to dark that Sunday when the Judge offered Mac a ride back to town, which he accepted. On the ride down, the Judge had skillfully drawn from Mac the circumstances of his coming to Ute City. He also caught a hint of Mac's love of the outdoors, its animals, birds, fish, and their habits. Next day while Mac was working after school, the Judge stopped at his house, chatted with his mother, and left a package. It turned out to be a fly rod, with reel, line, leaders, and flies.

It was a strange companionship that blossomed thereafter. Mac became friends with Sam, whom he had barely known in school, and who did not share his father's love of the outdoors. When Mac graduated from high school, it was Judge Lillard who wrangled a scholarship for him at the State University, where Mac was to study all those courses that could teach him more about the world he loved — biology, botany, forestry, and game management. When Mac was on vacation during his college days, the Lillard house was a second home.

There was never any doubt in Mac's mind as to what he wanted to be, and upon graduation he took a job with the Game and Fish Department. It took him five years, during which period his mother died, part of them spent in hated administrative work in distant parts of the state, before he was transferred to his present district. He suspected that Judge Lillard, a friend of politicians and a member of the State Game and Fish Commission, had something to do with the transfer. When charged with it, the Judge laughingly denied it. In a manner of speaking, Mac thought, he was a product of Judge Lillard's making.

Half an hour later Mac picked up the highway, which was slick with new snow and turned back toward Ute City. It was beginning to get dark now and Mac switched on his lights. A hundred useless speculations haunted his mind. Had the Judge suffered? Had Hutch been with him when he died? Mac tried to force himself to halt these speculations, but it was useless and only added to his stunned grief.

It was full dark when he turned off onto the Officer's Creek Road. His headlights shining through the still falling snow showed that there had been much traffic ahead of him. A couple of jeeps and a pick-up passed him, and then he saw a pair of lights topped by a red flashing light coming toward him through the snow. State Patrol? he wondered; and then as the lights passed him he saw the long black body of the Ute City Mortuary's hearse-ambulance. Mac knew bleakly that it held the body of his beloved friend.

It was another hour before Mac, slipping and sliding on the glassy road, pulled his pick-up into the barn lot of the Horn ranch. By his headlights Mac saw half a dozen jeeps and other vehicles pulled up at the fence, one of them the sheriff's white sedan topped by its red light. He also recognized Sam's foreign-make sedan.

Switching off his lights, Mac stepped down

into the slushy barn lot and headed for the house. At his knock, Mrs. Horn opened the door. She was a plain, pleasant, middle-aged woman who was wearing a pair of men's levis and a heavy sweater.

"Come in, Mac," she said quietly. Mac took off his hat and stepped into the big kitchen. He was surprised to see Jessie, an apron over her dress, at the big coal range stirring something on the stove. When she looked over her shoulder Mac saw that her eyes were red from weeping and that grief was stamped on her usually merry face.

"Sam's in there, Mac," Jessie said. She tipped her head toward the door of the adjoining room from which a murmur of men's voices issued.

Mac tramped across the linoleum and went through the door to the living room. Sam, Hutch, the sheriff, and three of the sheriff's part-time deputies and Mrs. Horn's ranch-hand were all seated there, on the sofa and the chairs.

Without speaking, Mac crossed to Sam and held out his hand. Sam stood up and took it. There was nothing Mac could say, and Sam knew it. It was useless to tell Sam he loved the old boy, that he considered him a father to him, that he was appalled at the death, or that Sam had his heartfelt sympathy, because Sam knew all these things already.

"You took your damn time," Sheriff Cosby said.

As always when he had any dealings with Frank Cosby, Mac had to keep a rein on his temper. To begin with, each disliked the other, and Cosby's manner of speaking, seldom polite, had an especially abrasive quality in talking with Mac.

"In case you don't know it, it's snowing outside," Mac said dryly.

There was dislike in the sheriff's pale eyes, but he ignored the jibe. "There's one thing I didn't tell you over the radio." He turned to Hutch Cameron. "Tell him, Hutch."

Hutch said quietly, "The Judge was murdered, Mac."

Mac's lips formed the question — Murdered? — but no sound came.

Hutch nodded, "Couldn't be anything else, Mac. The first shot went through his leg and killed his horse. Whoever it was shot him, came up about ten yards from him, then shot him in the chest and killed him. The first shot could've been a mistake, but the second — " Hutch's voice trailed off.

"But why? Why?" Mac demanded. "The Judge never had an enemy." He looked at Sheriff Cosby.

Frank Cosby's young face never looked

tougher or more angry. "Hutch thinks the Judge recognized the man who shot him. Rather than face the music, he killed the Judge, figuring nobody would know who did it."

Mac felt an almost uncontrollable wrath rising inside of him. It did not make sense that a man would kill another man rather than accept punishment for what must have been an accident. After a moment's reflection Mac said, "I won't buy that, Frank. Nobody's that crazy. Will you buy it?"

"I've already bought it," the sheriff said flatly. "If that isn't the way it happened, then we've got to assume that someone who hated the Judge hunted him out, shot his horse first, and then killed him. The chances of finding the Judge alone in that country are a million to one, I'd say."

Mac looked at Sam. "What d'you think, Sam?"

"I'm like Frank. I guess I have to, Mac."

At that moment Jessie stepped through the doorway. "Have you had anything to eat, Mac?" When Mac said he had not, Jessie said, "Your supper's ready."

Mac followed her out of the room with the sheriff trailing him. He saw the place set for him on the oilcloth-covered table, pulled out a chair, and sat down. The sheriff slacked into the chair opposite and they both were silent as Jessie at the stove filled Mac's plate with steak, potatoes, string beans.

As she set it before him, Mac said, "What're you doing here, honey?"

"Frank asked me if I wouldn't come along to help Mrs. Horn. He said there'd be a lot of people here and it wasn't fair for them to camp on her."

Mac took her hand and squeezed it gently. "I'm glad you came."

"And I'm glad *you* came," Jessie said softly.

Looking up, Mac saw the tears beginning to film her eyes, and some of her misery was communicated to him. The Judge, Mac knew, had been more than an employer to Jessie. He had been the friend who stepped in after her father's death to comfort her and her mother and to straighten out the tangled estate Abel Morfitt left. In a way she was much closer to the Judge than she had been to her father.

Jessie turned back to the stove for the coffee pot and Mac began eating.

"What d'you plan to do, Frank?" Mac asked after he had swallowed his first bite of food.

"That's a college boy's question for sure," Cosby said derisively. "I'll do what any sheriff would do. Tomorrow Hutch and I are going back to dig the slug out of that dead horse. Hutch says there's no exit hole. Meanwhile, you and the rest of my deputies will hit every hunting camp in the area. You'll check the guns and serial numbers and ask each man to stop in when he's through hunting so we can take a ballistics test."

"Can you force a ballistics test if the owner doesn't consent?"

The sheriff said grimly, "A court order will take care of any refusal."

Jessie came over and poured both men a cup of coffee, then sat down at the third chair.

"Where's Mrs. Horn?" Mac asked.

"She went to bed, Mac. She was an old, old friend of the Judge, too." Jessie looked at the sheriff. "How can you possibly know where these hunting camps are, Frank?"

"We'll just have to hunt them out."

Mac looked up from his plate. "I've got an idea, Frank. Why don't we get our Department plane to fly over tomorrow and spot the camps? They can call their locations to you on your radio or mine."

The sheriff looked dubious and Mac knew that he was trying to find some flaw in this suggestion, simply because it came from him. However, Frank Cosby was a good sheriff and Mac knew that his suggestion would be accepted.

"That'll save time," Frank conceded. "I've already called the Jamestown police to put a man on the Jamestown road. He'll take names and serial numbers. I've got Drew Morgan doing the same thing at the end of this road. If you'd been going the other way, he'd have stopped you."

"The weather man says clear tomorrow. I hope he's right," Mac said.

Now Frank stood up. "We'll bunk down in the living room, Mac. Jessie'll sleep in Mrs. Horn's room. I don't suppose you brought a sleeping bag?"

"I always carry one."

"Well, I'll go get mine," Frank said. He stepped out into the night as Mac drank the last of his coffee and rose, looking around the room. "Where's the phone, Jessie?"

"In the living room," Jessie said.

Mac went back into the living room, where he saw a wall phone. Looking at his watch, he saw that it was nine o'clock. Then he took a small address book from his shirt pocket, hunted up the number, and put in a long-distance call to the home of the Department head in Granite Junction, some two hundred miles away. The talk of Sam and the others trailed off so Mac could hear over the phone. The gruff voice of Joe Ormsby answered, and Mac, after explaining his reasons, made his request for the plane.

"I heard about the Judge over the radio tonight," Joe said. "Terrible thing, Mac. I know he was an old friend of yours."

"Oldest and the best," Mac said.

"Well, we'll take off as soon as it's light and fly up the Officer's Creek Road until we spot the Horn ranch. Have you got a map of that country, Mac?"

"In the pick-up," Mac said.

"Then we shouldn't have any trouble getting together over the radio. I'll be talking to you in the morning, Mac. So long." Mac hung up and returned to the kitchen.

Jessie was waiting for him and she said, "I'm going to bed, Mac. Kiss me good night."

She came into his arms and Mac said, "Why, you're trembling, honey."

"I have been since this afternoon, Mac. I just can't stop." She pulled Mac's head down and kissed him on the mouth. Then she said good night, turned, and went into Mrs. Horn's bedroom.

Later that night Chuck Daily pulled up on a country road several miles west of Ute City. He had found what he was looking for — a haystack well away from a ranch house and close to the road. He turned his jeep spotlight on the haystack and saw five deer feeding on the hay through a sagging barbed-wire fence that protected it. They turned to look at the light and their eyes glowed like sapphires. Slowly they began to move and Chuck drew a bead with his 270 on a buck moving away from him. He shot and the buck went down. Chuck switched off his spotlight. It was only a matter of minutes, even in the dark, for Chuck to skin out the deer, drag it under the fence, and load it into his jeep, covering it with a dirty tarp.

Back in town he backed up to his shed, dragged the deer across its dirt floor, pulled down the rope from a block and tackle, and strung up the deer by its hind legs. He was careful to tag the rack. Then he spread the ribs with a stick so that air could dry out the flesh.

He patted the hide affectionately. *You're my alibi, baby,* he thought.

Afterwards, Chuck moved a couple of barrels of trash from the corner of the dirt-floored shed, then with an axe and shovel he dug a trench several inches deep where the barrels had been. Taking his 30.06, a half-box of cartridges, and the two empty shells, he wrapped them all in a tarp and put them in the trench.

By the time he was through tamping the dirt back over the gun, it was impossible to tell where it was buried. He moved the barrels back and dropped the extra dirt into the barrel and covered it.

The time now was past 3:30 in the morning. Chuck checked his pockets to make sure he had enough shells for his 270, then climbed in the jeep, and went out in the darkness to head for his old camp.

III

Everyone in the Horn household was awake long before daylight. By dawn they were finished with the breakfast that Jessie and Mrs. Horn had cooked. While Mac rolled up his sleeping bag, the sheriff went out to his car to warm up his radio in preparation for reception.

When Mac stepped out of the door heading for his pick-up to stow away the sleeping bag, he saw that the six-inch snow was over and that the day would be clear and cold. The last stars sparkled icily as day came on. Even now jeeps and pick-ups with their headlights on were passing the Horn ranch, heading for the flat-top country. Traffic to the high hunting country had roused him several times during the night, and Mac knew these were hunters changing hunting grounds or camps.

He started the pick-up and turned the radio on, then took the map from the glove compartment and headed for Frank's car. As he walked toward it, he felt the old wariness that he always felt when meeting or talking with

Cosby. Although it had never been stated, both men knew why they disliked each other. It was simply that both men had courted Jessie when she came to work for the Lillards. Mac had resented every date she gave Frank; and every date she gave Mac was resented by Frank. They made no pretense of friendship; they were on the male's deadly business of winning a mate. When Jessie chose Mac over Frank, he had never forgiven Mac; and Mac, in turn, still resented the torment Frank had put him through.

When he reached Frank's car, Mac climbed into the front seat and extended the map. Frank opened it, looked at it, and handed it back. "You're the college boy, you mark it," he said.

"That joke is getting pretty weary, Frank," Mac said quietly. "Sam went to college. D'you call him 'college boy'? Jessie went to college. D'you call her 'college girl'?"

Frank looked at him stonily. "I like them."

Mac leaned back and regarded Cosby with puzzlement. "You must be part Indian, Frank. You never forgive nor forget, do you?"

"I do with some people," Frank said coldly.

"But it's over," Mac said quietly. "I'm engaged to Jessie and you're married."

"And to the wrong girl," Frank said bitterly. "Go on, mark your map."

Now Sam, Jessie, Hutch, and three deputies stepped out into the morning and headed for the sheriff's car.

"I'll have Jessie take down what the pilot says, so there's no chance for a mistake," Mac said.

"Good idea," Frank conceded. Mac stepped out of the car and headed for the pick-up, calling, "Come with me, Jessie."

Mac halted and watched her approach. He guessed that a night's rest had helped her recover from the state of shock she had been in last night. She seemed sad and subdued, which was only normal after her shock, but when he had hugged her this morning he noticed she was no longer shivering. Now, with the cold air, her cheeks took on their usual color. Jessie came up and linked her arm in Mac's as they headed for the pick-up.

"You think this will really work, Mac?"

"I don't see why not. My map has grids and so will the pilot's." He looked down at her. "You think you could take down what the pilot says in shorthand, Jessie.?"

"If I can hear him, of course." Then she said in a low voice, "Mac, we've *got* to make this work. We've *got* to find who killed the Judge."

"We will, Jessie. We will if it takes all the rest of our lives."

Mac helped Jessie into the pick-up, whose heater made the cab almost too warm. Then he drove a little ways across the barn lot so that he and the sheriff could not hear each other's radios. Mac offered Jessie a cigarette, lit one himself, and lowered the window. The radio was crackling with a fair amount of static. Mac handed his clip-board with attached pen to Jessie.

Suddenly the radio blasted on with a roar. "93 calling 77. Do you hear me?"

"Loud and clear," the sheriff answered.

Jessie asked, "Can't you turn it down a little, Mac? This'll blow us out of the cab."

Mac was turning down the volume as the voice came again. "77, I'm making a turn up the Officer's Creek Road. Can you give me the grid number where you are?"

Mac picked up the transmitter and said, "We are in G-4." There was a pause, and then the voice said, "Got it."

Mac turned to Jessie. "They'll be over in a few minutes." He cranked down the window on his side and stuck his head out, peering at the sky.

It was only a matter of minutes before the Department's silver single-engined monoplane grew from a speck to a noisy machine that thundered low over the ranch building, tilting its wings in a signal that the pilot had recognized the sheriff's car and the Department's pick-up. The plane rose and circled once while the pilot waved and then took off to the north. Soon the voice spoke over the radio. "There's a big tent on Lion's Creek. 6-1."

And so it went for the next hour as the plane made ever-widening circles over the flat-top country. In all, there were thirteen camps of varying sizes reported in, and Mac marked each one on his map as Jessie took down the pilot's every word. Mac figured from the scale on his map that the pilot had covered an area within a thirty-mile radius of where the Judge's body was found. It even included the high mountains over which nobody could travel in the snow that had fallen.

Half an hour later the plane roared over the ranch again and the radio voice said, "That's it, and good hunting!"

Mac turned the radio off, then drove the pick-up over to the sheriff's car. Sam had sat beside the sheriff during the radio talk while the three deputies were putting chains on their jeeps. Hutch was saddling the horses that he and Cosby would use to go to the Judge's dead horse. Mac and Jessie climbed in the back of the car and Mac leaned over Cosby's shoulder, pointing out the camp locations on the map the sheriff now had.

"Which ones were the big camps, Jessie?"

Referring to her notes, Jessie told him and Frank marked them down. Sam sat silently listening and watching.

As they were finishing, Hutch and the others came up to the car. The sheriff stepped out, spread the map on the hood, and with Mac looking over his shoulder, divided up the camp sites among the group. The three deputies, all local ranchers down the valley, knew the country and they quickly identified the camp locations for Mac.

The sheriff said, "You take the map, Mac. I won't need it because Hutch will be my guide." To the group in general he said, "You'll likely be able to drive into every camp. Remember, take the name and address of every hunter in each camp, along with the make, serial number, and caliber of each rifle."

Then he added wryly, "We might as well get set up to spend a couple of days at this. Most of these hunters will be out during the daylight hours. If any man objects to giving you his name or letting you take the serial number of his rifle, or doesn't want to come in to my office so we can shoot his gun, you can tell them this: A court order will get their guns even if they live out of state. Oh yes, and get the license number of every vehicle."

He paused, then went on. "Remember, as deputies you have the same power as the sheriff, only don't throw your weight around. Now let's get moving. Maybe we'll find some of them still in camp."

The deputies scattered to their jeeps, started their motors and pulled out of the snowy barn lot, the chains on their front wheels clanking rhythmically. They turned left at the gate and headed for their assignments.

Sam Lillard, wearing borrowed galoshes, sheepskin, and cap, approached the car. Jessie got out and came up to Mac as he was pocketing the map.

Sam said, "I'm coming with you, Mac."

Sam still wore a strip of tape across his nose which had been freshly applied this morning. His usually plump face seemed haggard and gray. Mac guessed that he had spent a rougher night than any of them.

"You don't have to, Sam. I can do this alone."

"I want to go," Sam said. "Sometimes you can look at a man and know if he's hiding something. At least I can in court, so why not here?"

"Take him along, Mac," Jessie said. "There's nothing for him to do around here except sit."

"True enough." Mac said. "Let's go get our

sleeping bags, Sam."

Jessie waited for them in the cold morning, pacing the barn lot to keep warm. In the far corral she saw the sheriff and Hutch leading their horses out through the gate. She watched them mount and ride off across the pasture, and she wondered dismally if this search would turn up the killer. New hunters would be coming in for days and old hunters going out. How would they know which was which? They would have to rely on the information the spotter in the plane had given them. But what if the killer had walked into the country, shot the Judge, and walked out again? He did not necessarily have to keep to the roads, and the storm would have hidden him until he was well out of the area. It all seemed so chancy and difficult.

Sam and Mac came out of the house with their sleeping bags and Jessie met them at the pick-up.

Jessie said, "Sam, I'll drive into town today and take care of the mail. I'll be back in time to help Mrs. Horn with supper. Is there anything you want me to do?"

"You might call Father Nick about the service, Jessie. I know he'll assume we want him, but I think we should ask him. Tell him I sent you."

Jessie nodded. "Good hunting, both of you."

Mac leaned down and kissed her, then circled the pick-up and climbed behind the wheel. Catching sight of his face in the rear-view mirror, he felt a sudden shock. He looked more like a hound, and a sad one, than ever. Here he had been concerned about Jessie's and Sam's looks, but now he had discovered that he looked every bit as haggard.

Sam climbed in and after waving good-bye to Jessie, Mac wheeled the pick-up out of the barn lot, turned left, and was soon in the timber.

Harve Wallis, after three months as Frank Cosby's deputy, still resented the fact that he was more office boy and errand boy than a working deputy. He, not Frank, should be the one working on Judge Lillard's murder. In the years since he had been an MP in Korea, he had worked as a deputy sheriff and once as a state patrolman before he was dismissed for molesting a woman speeder he had stopped. In all these jobs he had been a working sheriff, to all intents and purposes. Why, he reflected now, some of the sheriffs he had worked for lived in business suits and never carried a gun. Frank, however, was his own sheriff.

Harve was seated at the desk behind the counter that bisected the big sheriff's office on a front first-floor corner of the courthouse.

On the desk was a heap of mail he had picked up at the post office a few minutes ago. Behind the desk were files, a typewriter on a stand, and a glassed-in gun rack holding a variety of weapons, from a sub-machine gun to pistols.

Clumsily Harve started to sort the mail into three piles — an official pile for Frank, a personal pile for Frank and his wife, and his own. When he had finished, he shuffled through the half-dozen letters addressed to him and then tossed them aside, swearing under his breath. None of them was from Texas, and the Texas letter was the one he was looking for. His father's will was being probated, and each day for a month Harve had been expecting a notice that, as his father's sole heir, he would inherit the small ranch located in an obscure Texas county. Something, and he could guess what, was holding it up. The banks or some individuals probably had papers against the property and were getting theirs before he got his. His cousin Abe, a lawyer in a windy crossroads county seat, had written him to stay away until the estate was settled. That suited Harve perfectly. He did not want to return inheriting a flock of money demands and suits with their attendant grudges, which in that part of the country could grow into wicked family feuds.

His reverie was interrupted as someone entered the office. Looking up, he saw Selena standing in the doorway. Probably because she had been shopping this morning, her hair was combed, her dress neat, and she looked pretty.

"Dinner's ready, Harve."

"Be right down," Harve said, smiling. He watched her disappear and his smile vanished. *How about that,* he wondered. Had she dressed up for him because Frank was gone? When he first began boarding with them, because Selena wanted the money, he and Frank came down to the noon meal to find her slopping around in slippers and a baggy housedress. Those were the days when she was sullen and almost hostile to him. Lately, however, she had become almost embarrassingly friendly. Today would be the first time for a long while that they had eaten without Frank. And he had observed lately that under the surface of the relationship between Frank and Selena there was a coolness and resentment.

He got up and skirted the counter. As he locked the door he felt the hunter's sense of anticipation. She would not be the first married dame he had seen play around, if only to spite a husband.

Downstairs in the basement apartment

where the lights burned day and night for lack of windows, Harve went on through the living room to the kitchen. Selena was standing at the stove, dishing out the food, her back to him, and he eyed her appreciatively. She had good legs, and even if she was a little plump, he liked girls with some meat on their bones.

Well, here goes, he thought. Crossing to the stove, he put both hands on Selena's bare upper arms and kissed her neck just below the hairline. Selena shivered involuntarily and said, "Cut it out now, Harve."

No scream anyway, so Harve spun her around and tried to kiss her. She turned her head away, but Harve cupped her chin in his big hand, turned her face toward him, and kissed her. It was anything but a friendly kiss, and when she could, Selena pulled away. There was a hint of anger in her eyes as she said, "Harve, you got to quit that. If Frank knew, he'd shoot you."

Harve was experienced enough to know that if she really resented his kissing her, she would have belted him across the face. She really liked it, he thought; she was just a little scared of what kissing might lead to. He knew, and she knew, what it would lead to, but there was no sense rushing things. He had a whole month to make it happen, and it would. No use forcing it.

"Frank wouldn't shoot me over a kiss," Harve said. "Besides, you look so damn pretty I couldn't help it."

Selena flushed with pleasure and Harve thought he had better leave it on that note. He let go of her and, passing, patted her fanny. There was no reaction other than a protesting giggle.

Sitting down at the table, he waited until Selena brought their loaded plates and poured coffee. When she had sat down, she said, "Frank didn't call this morning, did he? He wouldn't, of course, but I just wondered."

"No. He's headed for the Judge's horse to see if they can find the bullet. Jessie Morfitt called in."

"You hear anything from home today?" Selena asked.

"Not a word," Harve said with disgust. "You don't know what these Texas courts can be like."

"If I had a ranch waiting for me, no court could keep me off it."

Harve shook his head. "They could if the sheriff was your dead daddy's creditor."

"Frank'd never do that," Selena said.

Harve looked at her and grinned. "No he wouldn't. He's too soft. They got a different kind of sheriff and a different kind of court in Texas."

"You just going to sit and wait here?" Selena asked.

"Oh, I'll give them another month. I told Frank I'd stay on through Thanksgiving."

They ate in silence until Selena noticed Harve's plate was empty. She rose, got him seconds, and returned to the table. Harve wolfed down his second helpings, then pushed his plate away, drew out a sack of tobacco dust, and rolled a smoke. Selena had already lighted a cigarette.

When Harve had lighted his cigarette, he said, "Going to hate to see me go, baby?"

Selena blushed. "I'll live," she said.

"You mean you won't miss me?"

"I didn't say that," Selena said. "Sure, I'll miss you. At least you give me a laugh once in a while and at least you treat me like a woman."

"And Frank doesn't?"

Selena looked searchingly at him and was about to say something when she thought better of it. She rose, saying, "Skip it, Harve. Go and turn the TV on. I'll be in after I get this mess cleaned up."

Hutch and the sheriff came upon the Judge's dead horse in the late morning. Hutch had taken a shorter route than the roundabout way past his camp. They tied their horses well away from the dead horse and then tramped through the six inches of snow to halt by the carcass. Yesterday, when Hutch returned with the pack horse, he had first turned the animal over with two ropes and the aid of both horses. He, too, had been thinking of retrieving the bullet from the gun that killed the Judge. Now he toed the horse's rump and found it stiff and frozen. He leaned over, put his hand on the ribcage, and said, "The slug went in about here on the other side, Frank. There's where the heart lies. I reckon the slug will be either in the heart or against the ribs on this side."

Frank nodded. "Well, let's get at it."

Hutch had a cased hatchet hanging from his belt, and now he took it out and started to work. Cutting through the ribs, he opened a window into the horse's chest and folded back the flap of the ribs and skin. Both men leaned over and examined the ribs.

"Look there, Frank. That rib is nicked from the inside."

"Should be between the rib and the hide then, Hutch." Hutch folded the flap back in place, drew out his hunting knife, and felt with his big hand along the hide that covered the ribs. When he felt an alien body under the skin, he slit the hide, reached in, and drew out a mushroomed, bloody slug. Reaching down in the snow, he washed the blood from the bullet, and held it up for the other man's inspection.

Cosby examined it in silence for a moment, noting that the bullet had mushroomed, but noting also that a quarter-inch of the butt end of the bullet retained its shape. This quarter-inch was enough to identify the killer's gun through a ballistics test.

"Looks like a thirty-ought-six, Hutch."

"That's what I think."

The sheriff unbuttoned his red jacket, slipped the slug in his shirt pocket, and buttoned the pocket flap carefully.

"Want to see that footprint I covered?" Hutch asked.

"We won't need it now, Hutch. Not with this." He patted his pocket.

A look of disappointment came over Hutch's usually taciturn face, and Frank felt a little ashamed of himself. He had not told Hutch that in case they could not recover the bullet they would take the print.

"It's this way, Hutch. We've got the bullet, so we don't need the print. These print casts can't tell the FBI much. The Bureau could probably tell us what company made the boots and that's about all. Even if the company had records of shipments to stores in this area, it would be an impossible job for the stores to remember who bought boots from them in the last three or four years."

"Yeah, I can see that," Hutch said.

"There were probably fifty hunters tramping around in this area this morning, and very likely thirty are wearing the same make of boots that Bill Miller sold them. Looks pretty hopeless, Hutch."

Hutch nodded, accepting this, and said, "Well, let's go shovel out my jacket."

Mac and Sam noted the spot where Chuck Daily's jeep had turned off on the mining road; however, they wanted to reach the most distant camps first. Once Mac stopped, consulted his maps, checked the speedometer, and went on. Presently the wood road forked. There were new tracks on the right-hand fork and drifted-over tracks on the left-hand fork. The latter fork headed in the direction of a camp location the spotter had given him. Mac turned down it, shifting into low, low. They traveled approximately three miles before they came into a clearing in the timber, on the edge of which a tent was pitched. A jeep was pulled off under some trees.

"Isn't that George Maxwell's jeep, Mac?"

"I think it is," Mac said. There was no need for him to tell Sam that Bill Geary was probably with George. He would find out soon enough anyway.

Mac got out of the pick-up and headed for the tent. A lot of hunters, he knew, would only hunt in the morning and evening hours when the game was astir, counting hunting in the middle of the day a waste of time. Mac hoped Bill and George held these views.

He prowled around the camp, saw no game hanging, and started back to the pick-up. Then he halted and cocked his head. He heard something and listened intently. Then the faint sound of voices came to him and he knew that he was in luck.

Mac was standing in front of the tent when George Maxwell pulled into sight with Bill. For a moment Mac felt a stir of apprehension. What would Sam say when he saw Geary?

Now both men saw Mac and waved to him. As they came closer, George Maxwell called, "Don't shoot, Mac. We'll turn over to you every darn deer track we found."

Mac heard the cab door slam and looked over his shoulder. Sure enough, Sam had recognized Bill Geary and was about to join the group.

Bill and George halted by Mac. "You snooping for licenses, Mac, or just looking for a handout?" Bill asked. He shoved his red cap to the back of his head and there was a friendly smile on his black-Irish face. Then both men caught sight of Sam plodding toward them. Bill Geary's face altered slightly, but George's round face showed pleasure. He was a friendly man, and for the moment he either forgot or did not care about Bill's quarrel with Sam.

Mac said easily, "I got me a helper, George."

"Hi, Sam," George called. "Are you Mac's deputy now?"

Sam came up, nodded to Geary, and said. "I guess you could call it that, George."

Mac knew it was time to take over. "George, there was a hunting accident near here yesterday and the sheriff has taken over. He's deputized several of us to check the guns in the hunting camps. You were camped opening day, weren't you?" George nodded, a puzzled look on his face.

"You don't mind if we take the serial numbers of your guns? We know your names and addresses, so that won't be necessary. Mind you, you don't have to give me the serial number, George, but if you refuse, I know Frank can get a court order."

"Why should I object?" George said, and he extended his rifle. "Here."

Mac accepted the rifle, took out his notebook, and copied down the serial number. Then Bill Geary spoke for the first time.

"Who got hurt, Mac?"

"Not hurt, murdered, Bill," Mac said quietly. "It was Judge Lillard. He was shot twice."

Mac looked up to find Sam watching Geary. His face was impassive, but his eyes were alert, intent.

"My God!" George exclaimed. "The Judge is dead?"

"I'm afraid so, George. Whoever killed him left the scene."

"Sam, I'm sorry as hell," George said. "That's awful, simply awful! I just can't believe it!"

"I'm sorry too, Sam," Bill Geary said stiffly. There was the beginning of anger, though, in his face. "I see why you've come to our camp, Mac. You think I killed the Judge."

Mac said patiently, "Bill, have we even suggested any such thing? Did you see a plane flying over this morning?"

"We saw it," George said.

"That plane was spotting all the camps within a thirty-mile radius. We're taking the serial numbers of all the guns in all the camps and asking the hunters to drop by the sheriff's office so that the guns can be fired for a ballistics test." Mac looked at Geary and Maxwell. "Believe me, you two aren't singled out any more than thirty other hunters."

"Like hell I'm not!" Bill Geary said hotly. "Everybody knows I tied into the Judge and Sam. It looks like you've already made up your minds!"

Sam said, "That's absurd, Bill. I, for one, didn't even know you were hunting here. I don't think Mac and the sheriff knew either. Did you, Mac?"

"No, and Frank didn't either or he'd have mentioned it."

Bill put out his hand. "Let me see your notebook, Mac."

Mac offered him the open notebook. Bill glanced at it, then turned to the previous page.

"Your story won't wash, Mac. You haven't taken any other gun numbers — you've only got George's and you're hoping to get mine." He handed back the notebook.

Mac thumbed his Stetson to the back of his head and reached deep into his reservoir of patience. "Bill, yours was just the first camp we've come to."

"Just a coincidence, eh?" Bill asked sardonically. "Well, I don't believe it was a coincidence." He looked hotly at Sam. "I can see the lot of you deciding that because I hated the Judge I killed him."

Mac said, still patiently, "Bill, there's a quick way to prove that you didn't kill him.

Submit your gun for a ballistics test. It'll prove your innocence or — " He stopped.

"Or guilt," Bill finished for him. "Why don't you say it?"

"Or guilt," Mac said. "It's bound to prove one or the other, isn't it?"

"Go on! Why don't you ask if I went hunting alone yesterday?"

Mac's voice showed a trace of irritation as he answered. "Bill, I'm not questioning you. I couldn't if I wanted to. I haven't got the authority."

"You said it," Bill Geary said. "You haven't got the authority. You admit I don't have to show you my gun. All right, I won't!"

Mac saw the open distress on George's face as Bill stopped talking and his glance shuttled to Sam. There was a stony suspicion reflected there, and Mac admitted to himself that he too was not only puzzled, but perhaps suspicious.

George said, almost vehemently, "Bill, don't you see what you're doing? You're drawing attention to yourself by refusing to give Mac the number of your gun."

Bill only grinned at him.

Mac said reasonably, "It's now or later, Bill. Can't you see that?"

Bill said with a wry humor, "What you're saying is, why buck city hall, isn't it?"

Mac nodded, "Something like that."

Bill sighed. "It's just that I think my rights have been trampled on enough, for one thing, Mac." Then he held out his rifle, saying, "I guess I can take a little more stomping."

Mac noted the make, caliber, and serial number of Bill's gun in his notebook and then returned it to him. "Much obliged, Bill. When you two get through hunting, will you drop your guns off at the sheriff's office so he can fire them for a test bullet?"

They said they would, and Mac and Sam tramped back through the snow to the pickup. As Mac turned the vehicle around, Sam gazed stonily ahead of him, his eyes unseeing.

Mac said in a tone of exasperation, "Bill Geary can be the orneriest human alive."

Sam was silent a long moment, then he said quietly, "He did it, Mac."

Mac swerved his head and looked at Sam. "That's an odd statement, coming from a lawyer."

"If he didn't do it, why didn't he hand his gun over without a fuss, like George did?"

"Because he's Bill Geary. There's an easy way and a hard way to do everything. Bill always likes the hard way."

"I think he did it," Sam repeated. "It was plain in his face."

"It was plain that he thought he was being

discriminated against. But did you think you saw guilt in his face, Sam?"

"I did," Sam said flatly. "Didn't you?"

"I did not," Mac said just as flatly. "He's just sore at the world, Sam, and your being with me made him suspicious."

Sam only grunted.

Mac looked obliquely at Sam and said, "Sam, can I ask you a question that I shouldn't?"

"You're going to anyway, so go ahead."

"All right. I know it's privileged information, Sam, but what went on at the Gearys' divorce trial?"

Sam looked at him swiftly. "You know better than to ask that, Mac."

"It's over and done with, but if it's messy I don't want to know."

Sam pondered this and a bitterness was reflected in his broad face. "After yesterday I don't see why I should do Bill the favor of keeping my mouth shut." He looked at Mac. "But will you do me the favor of keeping yours shut?"

"You know I will."

Sam thought for a moment. "There was nothing at all messy about it, Mac. Oddly enough, the cause of the divorce was money — or the lack of it — non-support, you might say."

Mac frowned. "I thought Bill had a good

115

thing in that agency."

"He has. That's the funny part of it. Once when Bill was out of town, Lola went down to the office and went over his books." Sam paused, isolating what was coming next. "She found Bill was making twice the money he brought home. He didn't deny this to Judge Overman."

"What was he doing with it, then?"

"Gambling, he told the Judge. That, combined with the fact that he was away from home so much of the time, was Lola's basis for requesting a divorce."

Mac thought about this. He knew Bill had branch agencies in three small towns down the valley, but he could hit all of them in one day. As for gambling, that was possible, but only just possible.

"Sam," Mac asked, "d'you believe Bill's a heavy gambler?"

"He claimed that, Mac. I didn't. I think that's why Judge Overman was so rough on him in the property settlement." He looked at Mac. "He'll duck out, Mac. Mark my words."

Mac had no reply to this, although he did not believe it. Sam, Mac was thinking, couldn't be held accountable for his speech or actions today. The Judge's death was too close; so was Bill's attack on him and the Judge.

116

Mac followed his own tracks back toward the Horn ranch. When he came to the mine road where the fresh jeep tracks turned off, he slowed down and regarded the snow, noting that there were two sets of tracks, one fresh and one drifted track made just after the snow started yesterday. Then he turned off and followed the tracks. The pick-up had rough going when Mac had to leave the road and bushwhack. For a while he thought the truck would bog down and he would have to put on chains. However, the careening, skidding vehicle, mowing down the aspens and small spruce that barred the way, finally came to the edge of a park. Here he swung right and followed the jeep tracks crossing the park before he braked the truck to a stop. Chuck Daily had a fire going and was standing by it, hands on hips, regarding the pick-up, which he had heard approach. Mac stepped out into the snow along with Sam and both men walked toward the fire.

"Hi, Chuck."

"Hi ya, Mac. Hello, Sam. Have any trouble getting here?"

"Some," Mac said. He did not like Chuck Daily and had a hard time concealing it. He noted that Sam did not bother to return Chuck's greeting, and he remembered that Sam had represented a client in an unsavory money-demand suit against Chuck Daily.

Mac looked around the camp and spotted Chuck's battered jeep parked in the trees. A massive rack of a bull elk projected beyond the side of the jeep and Mac observed, "Looks like you had some luck, Chuck."

"Come look at it. I like to busted a gut skinning him out. I had to quarter him to load him."

The three of them tramped over to the jeep and regarded the severed head and a mountain of meat that almost overflowed the bed of Chuck's jeep.

"That's a big fellow, Chuck," Mac said.

"Ain't he though?"

Now that he was close to Chuck, Mac could smell the reek of whisky on his breath and the raw, acrid odor of sweat. He looked at Chuck's filthy, blood-stained clothes with a distaste he could scarcely conceal. A man cannot skin out and cut up a big elk without bloodying himself and his clothes, but Chuck's clothes had been filthy to start with.

"You fellows like a drink?" Chuck asked. "I got a bottle over there."

"No, thanks, Chuck," Mac said. "We've got to be getting on."

"Where are you heading for?" Chuck asked curiously.

"Right here, Chuck," Mac said. "I wonder

118

if you'd let me have a look at your gun and your license."

"Sure. But what for?" Chuck asked.

Sam, Mac noted, was studying Chuck's unshaven face, trying to probe behind the slyness that stamped it.

Mac answered easily. "There's been a shooting accident in this area, Chuck. A man was killed. The sheriff deputized some of us to take down the serial numbers of the guns of all the hunters who were in this area yesterday. Were you here yesterday?"

"Sure," Chuck said cheerfully. And then he frowned. "Why the serial numbers?"

"We're asking all the hunters we check to bring their guns into the sheriff so he can have a ballistics test made. Can I take the serial number of your rifle?"

"Hell, yes," Chuck said. He moved to the front seat of the jeep where his rifle lay across the seats. Picking it up, he said, "Here you are." Mac accepted the battered 270, took out his notebook, and copied down the serial number. Chuck offered his license next, and it was in order.

"This fellow run, I take it," Chuck said.

"That's right," Mac said, and then he remembered. He handed the rifle back to Chuck and said, "Thanks, Chuck. Will you drop by the sheriff's office and leave your gun there? It'll be returned to you after they fire a test bullet."

"Take it with you. I sure won't be needing it," Chuck said. "I got my deer yesterday and my elk today."

Mac looked around him at the surrounding trees.

"Where's your deer?"

"I took him to town yesterday morning," Chuck said. "He was a big one and I knew if I got an elk I couldn't take them both at the same time." He grinned, and Mac saw the twin row of rotted teeth behind Chuck's loose lips. "Looks like I figured right."

"I wondered about those two sets of tracks," Mac said. "What time did you go to town?"

"I got him at first light," Chuck said. "It started to snow while I was skinning him out."

"Well, you're all set for meat this winter, Chuck," Mac said. "I'll take your rifle if you want."

"I was just fixing to fry up a steak before I take off for town. I sure got plenty if you fellows will stay and eat."

"Thanks, Chuck. But we've got a lot of territory to cover today. I think we'd better get on."

Mac turned to Sam, and Chuck followed them past the campfire as they headed for the truck.

"Who was it got killed?" Chuck asked conversationally. Mac and Sam both halted and looked at him.

"It was Judge Lillard," Mac said.

Chuck's jaw slacked. "Not your dad, Sam?"

"Yes, Chuck," Sam said quietly.

"Oh, Lord! I'm sorry," Chuck said. "He was a fine man, Sam. The finest man in town."

"I agree with you, Chuck," Sam said gently.

"Well, I hope the sheriff finds who done it," Chuck said. He added then, as if to himself, "Just think, Judge Lillard is dead."

Sam, unable to bear with more commiseration, turned and walked over to the pick-up, and got in the cab.

"Thanks, Chuck. Be seeing you in town," Mac said.

Mac turned the pick-up around and started back in his own tracks. The going was much easier now.

Mac observed then, "Bill Geary could take a lesson in manners from Chuck."

"But not in cleanliness," Sam said wryly. He looked at Mac. "He's a known scoundrel, Mac. You know that."

"He's also one of the best hunters in the country, Sam. I think he'd know what he was shooting at."

"Well, he's got a lot of meat to prove it," Sam said.

Mac and Sam arrived back at Mrs. Horn's ranch after Hutch, the sheriff, Mrs. Horn, and Jessie had finished supper. Having completed the quizzing of their four assigned camps, they were more fortunate than the other deputies, who had not yet returned.

While the two men washed up, Jessie and Mrs. Horn laid out their supper on the big kitchen table at which Frank Cosby and Hutch kept their seats. When they were both seated and the food had been dished out, Cosby reached in his shirt pocket, took out the mushroomed bullet, and set it on the table. "We dug this out of the Judge's horse," he said.

Mac picked it up, looked at it, and said, "Thirty-ought-six?"

Cosby nodded. "Just before supper Hutch and I pulled a slug out of one of Hutch's cartridges. The butt end matches this for size." He put the slug back in his pocket and buttoned the flap. "What kind of a day did you have?"

"No trouble," Mac said. He was determined that he himself would not appear to prejudge Bill Geary.

But Sam spoke up. "What you mean, Mac, is that there was no *serious* trouble."

The sheriff looked from one man to the other, his face questioning.

Sam went on, "Bill Geary and George Maxwell were in the first camp we hit, Frank."

At the mention of Bill Geary's name, Jessie turned from the sink and crossed over to the table, wiping her hands on her apron.

"Bill Geary was hunting in the area opening day?" Jessie asked.

Sam nodded.

"What about Bill, Mac?" The sheriff asked.

"He thought we were singling him out for a suspect, Frank. We went round and round for a while until we convinced him the way to prove his innocence was to let his gun be fired."

"I think he's our man," Sam said quietly. "He had the motive, he had the hatred, and he looked guilty."

"So that's it," Jessie said softly, bitterly. "He was going to get even with the Judge at all costs."

The sheriff's face held an expression of impatience as he said curtly, "Tell me the whole story."

Mac did so, and accurately. When he was finished, Jessie said eagerly, "Are you going to arrest Bill tomorrow, Frank? Aren't those the actions of a guilty man?"

"On what grounds do I arrest him, Jessie?" Cosby asked.

Sam said, "Suspicion of murder."

But Frank said easily, "Sam, you're too good a lawyer to really mean that."

"I guess I am," Sam admitted. "Still, I feel he did it."

"Do you, Mac?" Frank asked.

Mac was silent a long moment. He had been expecting this question, and he had framed an answer to it. Sam, understandably, wanted to believe in Geary's guilt; so did Jessie, because Geary had assaulted both her employers. Feminine illogic plus her warm loyalty, when added to her genuine grief, dictated her answer. Now Mac looked at Jessie and he saw that she was more anxious than any of them to hear his answer.

"I don't think I do, Frank."

Jessie said hotly, but inaccurately, "He'd have killed Sam and the Judge in the courthouse if Frank hadn't stopped him!"

"I think he'd have liked to hurt them," Mac said.

"Anyone who'd do that is capable of murder," Jessie said.

The sheriff spoke quietly. "The proof, Jessie, the proof."

There was real anger in Jessie's gray eyes. "What more proof do you need? At first he wasn't going to let Mac take the serial number of his gun. He only gave in when he saw you'd get it anyway." She looked at Mac. "How else would a guilty man act? Sam's right!"

Frank said dryly, "Jessie, you can't judge a man from what his face tells you. That's what makes poker games."

He rose. "We'll wait for the ballistics tests."

IV

The funeral service for Judge Lillard was held on Wednesday at the Episcopal church in the older residential section. There were, of course, official deputations sent by the State Bar Association and the Judge's Masonic order. However, there were people from all over the state packed into the church — men who had known and liked the Judge when he was a state senator.

Chuck Daily was in attendance this day. He had shaved and bathed and borrowed a white shirt that had belonged to Minnie Gerber's husband. Minnie had had to tie his necktie, which had also belonged to her husband. In mismatched coat and pants, and wearing rough work shoes, Chuck Daily was better-dressed than he had been since the last time he wore a baby's dress.

Seated in a far corner of the last row of pews, Chuck only half listened to the funeral service. Never having been in church before, Chuck was unacquainted with the ritual of kneeling, but he took his cue from the others.

126

Midway through the service, Chuck began to wonder why he had come. Nobody would have noted his absence. Indeed, he was sure many people would wonder at his presence. Long ago he had put in a summer as yard man for the Lillards and eventually he had been fired for selling the Lillards' tools to buy wine. That, if anyone asked, was his reason for attending the funeral: he was an old employee of the Judge.

In reality, the reason Chuck attended the funeral was that he could not help himself. He had no sense of guilt for what he had done and no wish to atone for what he considered only an error of judgment; he was simply curious to see the end of an incident he himself had precipitated.

The service over, Chuck headed toward the business section of town. By now he was doubting the wisdom of attending the ceremony. If he had not shot the Judge, would he have attended the Judge's funeral, he asked himself. The answer was no. Then, in effect, he was calling attention to himself, and this was a mistake he had sworn not to make. He had already concluded that the smart thing to do was to go on living his life in exactly the same manner as he had lived it before the Judge's death. Blend in, don't stand out, don't talk about the Judge; do what you always do, he had told himself. But today his act of attending the funeral had not been normal.

He would have to be more careful.

At a grimy bar called the Elite — pronounced Elight by its patrons — Chuck turned in. It was a dark hole holding four tables, at the rearmost of which were seated three of the town's winos. They greeted Chuck without warmth as he went up to the scarred bar and leaned his elbows on it. There were no bar stools in the Elite because, as the proprietor had learned to his sorrow, they were too easy to fall off of, resulting in suits and threats of suits.

Mike Conti, the proprietor, and a neighbor of Chuck's, ambled up to Chuck. He was a bald, fat man in shirt sleeves, with a dirty apron tied around his waist. A wet, unlighted cigar was in the corner of his mouth. He did not have to ask Chuck what he wanted. He simply reached for a quart of muscatel, set a water glass in front of Chuck, poured it full, and put the bottle back.

"Where the hell are you going, all duded up?" Mike asked.

"Been to the Judge's funeral," Chuck said idly.

Mike's heavy eyebrows lifted. "You mean they let you in?"

Because Mike occasionally extended Chuck a couple of dollars' worth of credit, Chuck smiled at the joke. "They can't keep you out of a funeral, can they?"

"You was friends with the Judge?" Mike asked curiously.

Careful, Chuck thought to himself. "Oh, I worked for him on and off," Chuck said idly. "He was all right."

"Why you figure anyone would want to kill him?" Mike asked.

"Accident, prob'ly."

"Accident hell! Didn't you read the paper?"

Shut up, Chuck told himself. He took a drink of his wine and did not answer.

Mike turned to the winos and called, "Hey, listen to this. Chuck didn't even know the Judge was murdered."

One of the men at the table called, "Where you been, stupid?"

Chuck knew he had made another mistake besides attending the funeral. He was simply calling attention to himself again.

He gulped down the muscatel as if it were pop, put a dime on the counter, looked at Mike, and said in a surly voice, "A wise guy!" Then he turned and left the bar.

Unlike the State Highway Patrol, the Forest

Service, and the National Park Service, the Game and Fish Department, once they were satisfied with a man, seldom transferred him to a new area. Consequently, when Mac was transferred to Ute City, he waited about a year to see if the Department was satisfied with his work and he was sure it was, and then he bought himself a tiny one-bedroom Victorian house in the town's riverbottom — a house with gingerbread on the eaves and around the front porch.

Patiently he had repaired, refinished, and painted the little house. He bought some comfortable furniture and turned the living room into a library. Two walls were given over to books in bookcases shoulder high. Slowly he accumulated appliances for the kitchen. His bedroom was as spartan as a monk's cell.

Mac already knew by that time that he would have many callers and considerable paper work to do. Somehow the presence of callers, the need for files, desk, and typewriter, seemed to violate the privacy of his home. Accordingly, his next project had been to rehabilitate and floor the shed behind the house, add a garage, and move his office into the shed. The office consisted of a single room holding desk, chair, typewriter, and filing cabinets, and also a barrel stove and an easy chair. The walls were papered with maps of the area.

This morning, which was chill but sunlit, Mac, in a clean uniform, opened his office door and saw a slip of paper that had been pushed under it. Picking it up, he saw that it was an estimate of Harry Ashbaugh for re-roofing his office. Harry had penned at the bottom of the paper: *Call me if this estimate don't suit you. If it does, I'll be over tomorrow morning, Thursday.*

Thursday was today. Mac had not looked in on his office when he returned last night, and Harry had undoubtedly measured for his estimates yesterday and left the note. Well, the estimate seemed reasonable and Mac wadded up the paper and threw it in the wastebasket.

He swung his chair around, faced the typewriter, and while he was inserting the paper, carbon, and blue second sheet in the machine, he heard a truck drive up. He got up and went to the door and saw Harry Ashbaugh and his helper get out of their pick-up, to which was attached a two-wheeled tar boiler. Both men wore tar-spotted bib overalls over heavy jackets. The helper immediately began to lift out from the truck cylinders of cold tar which he tossed into the unlit boiler. Harry, a man in his late fifties with a weatherbeaten skin and friendly dark eyes, spotted Mac and came over to the door.

"Hi, Mac. The estimate all right?"

"Morning, Harry. Sure, seems reasonable enough."

"It wasn't supposed to," Harry said and grinned. "On these government jobs I pad hell out of everything."

Mac smiled too. "We expect that. Still, you're only over-charging us one-third. Usually it's one-half."

Harry laughed quietly and then his face sobered. "That was a mighty fine funeral they gave the Judge. There were even people standing outside. I had to."

"He had a lot of friends," Mac said simply.

"You figure there's anything to the talk that Frank Cosby and the Judge's closest friends suspect Bill Geary of killing the Judge?"

Mac tried to keep the alarm out of his voice as he asked, "Is there talk?"

"I've heard some. Fact is, I came close to getting in a fight over it. You don't do that at my age."

"Bill a special friend of yours?"

Harry nodded and said, "Guess you'd say so. We bowl together a lot."

Harry's helper now lighted the tar boiler and its roar made conversation impossible. Mac turned back into his office and closed the door, but he did not sit down. He stood there, feeling a sudden anger at Jessie and Sam. If there was talk around town that Bill Geary was suspected by the Judge's friends of his murder, then it could only stem from Sam and Jessie. Harry, who was no liar, could not have made this up.

On impulse then and still angry, Mac went into the garage, got in his pick-up, and drove down to the Lillard office.

Jessie was not in the reception room but, having heard the door slam, she appeared almost immediately. She gave Mac a searching look, then said, "Why, Mac, you look sort of grim this beautiful morning."

"I feel grim," Mac said. "Is Sam in his office?"

Jessie frowned, probably at his brusqueness, Mac thought.

"Yes, go on back."

"Lead the way," Mac said. "I want you there, too."

"What's got into you, Mac?" Jessie asked soberly.

"You'll find out."

Jessie led the way back to Sam's office, where Sam was studying a case book. When he saw Mac, he put a marker in the book, took off his glasses, and said, "Morning, Mac. What's new with you?"

Mac did not sit down and neither did Jessie.

"Something you won't like," Mac said.

Then he repeated Harry Ashbaugh's rumor regarding Bill Geary. "That rumor could've been started only because you two've talked."

Sam looked at Jessie. "I've thought Bill killed Dad, but I've never said it around town. Have you, Jessie?"

Jessie looked almost frightened. "Why, not that I remember. I've told you and Sam and Hutch and Frank what I think, but that's all."

Mac said evenly. "And Mrs. Horn, and Frank's deputies and Mrs. Johnson."

"You sound as if we aren't entitled to an opinion, Mac," Jessie said resentfully.

"Your boss is a lawyer and I'm not," Mac said. "Ask him what could happen if anyone heard you stating your opinion, Jessie."

"Touché," Sam said wryly. "If Bill Geary heard it, there would be a suit for slander and defamation of character, with judgments against us probably awarded." Sam closed his eyes, and, in the gesture of his father, he rubbed the bridge of his nose with thumb and index finger. "You're right, Mac. I guess I've been a little crazy these last few days."

"Well, I haven't!" Jessie said hotly. "I won't be scolded for saying what I think is true!"

"I'm not scolding you, I'm scared for you," Mac protested.

With feminine illogic, Jessie said, "You

think Bill's innocent, don't you?"

Mac said slowly, "I think he is, but I won't talk about it until the ballistics tests are in."

"Oh, don't express an opinion! That's dangerous!" Jessie said sardonically. "Now that the thought-control class is over, may I go now, teacher?"

She did not wait for Mac to speak but walked out of the room.

"Thanks, Mac," Sam said quietly. "I'm glad you heard this rumor before Bill Geary did. I assume he hasn't heard it or he'd probably be in here with a gun."

"Just hold tight, Sam. It won't be long before the ballistics reports are in. So long."

At the sound of his footsteps in the corridor, Jessie began typing. Mac came up silently behind her, lifted her raven hair, and kissed the back of her neck. She turned and looked up at him. "You're right, Mac. Damnit, you always are. I shouldn't have lost my temper."

"You're very pretty when you do," Mac said. "So long, honey."

Afterwards, out in the chill noon sunlight, Mac remembered he was past due for grocery shopping. He headed down the street toward the store through the scattering of foot traffic. The twelve o'clock rush of cars and people was over, so that it was easy to spot Cy Hartford half a block away. He was a rancher who had a place up the river, a heavy-set, bow-legged man with a rolling gait who could have been mistaken for a sea captain had he not been wearing a soiled Stetson, buttonless sheepskin coat, and manure-stained galoshes. As he approached Mac, his broad and ruddy face broke into a smile.

"Well," said Mac, "The Missus finally let you out, did she, Cy? How you been?"

The two men shook hands and Cy said, "Why aren't you up in the hills pinching hunters? I know you loaf most of the time, but don't you even work during hunting season?"

"Only every other day, Cy."

"And every other night?" Cy asked shrewdly.

Mac laughed. "Jessie doesn't come under the heading of work, Cy."

"Does catching spotlighters?" Cy asked.

"It does if I'm lucky," Mac said. "Why? You been having trouble?"

"Trouble?" Cy snorted. "Why, I invite them out to my place, Mac. The fewer deer, the more haystacks for me. If you game fellas would open it up to spotlighters, we could run twice the cattle we're running now, because we'd have twice the feed."

"You'd have a bunch of dead cows, too, Cy," Mac said. "Are they working out around you?"

136

Cy nodded. "A fellow woke me up the other night shooting. I just rolled over and went to sleep."

"When was this, Cy?"

The rancher, in an effort to recall, plucked at his full lower lip. "Let's see. It was Friday, the first day of hunting season. The next morning I found a pile of guts by the stack east of the place."

"Cy, do me a favor. Next time you hear one of these spotlighters, give me a call. I might be able to nail one."

Cy grinned. "Not me. They're my friends."

Mac had to smile. "You're a stubborn cuss, Cy. I hope they nail one of your horses some night. Then you'll change your tune."

"When that happens I might consider calling you, but not until then."

"Well, say hello to the Missus, Cy. I'll be out your way sometime."

"You stop in then, you hear?" Cy said. "I'll even give one of you deer herders a meal, so long as it's you."

They parted and Mac continued up the street. The strange thing about their conversation was that Cy Hartford had meant every word he said. Each year, but especially after a hard winter, the ranchers' organizations plead with the State to reduce the deer and elk herds which were eating their stacks and devouring their winter ranges.

As for catching the spotlighters, it was next to impossible. Out of season it was possible to get a warrant to search the premises of a man suspected of poaching. In season, however, when you had a perfect right to kill game, there was no way of knowing if it was shot illegally.

Still, Mac thought, I suppose I ought to take a look.

That noon, Sheriff Cosby took two rifles from a dozen stacked in the corner in his office. He consulted the tags hanging from the trigger guards to make sure he had Bill Geary's and George Maxwell's guns.

His first stop was at Bill Geary's apartment. There was no answer to his ring. It occurred to him then that since Bill was a bachelor now, he probably ate all his meals downtown. However, there was an off-chance that he might catch Bill at his insurance agency and he drove there next.

The Geary Insurance Agency occupied a one-story cinder-block office building on the west side of the town's business district, wedged between a laundry and a sporting goods store.

Frank locked the car and went into the agency. It held three desks behind the low railing; at one of them a girl was typing. At the sound of the door closing, she turned.

"Morning," Frank said. "Bill isn't around?"

"No, he isn't, Sheriff."

"Know where he usually eats?"

"At the Ute Grill, but you won't find him there today. I think he must be out of town."

Frank said evenly. "Did he tell you where he was going?"

The girl was plainly embarrassed now. "No, he called me the other night, mentioned two policies he wanted mailed out, and that's all. He didn't show up day before yesterday, or yesterday, or today."

"Does he usually tell you where he's going?"

"Yes. That's why this seems so strange."

"Well, if he gets in touch with you, I wonder if you'd give me a call. I have a gun of his and I'd like to drop it off at his apartment when he gets home."

The girl said she would, and the sheriff went out to his car. This was a little strange, Frank thought, and he was surprised that he felt a little envy. He could not remember the day when it would have been possible for him to pick up and take off without letting someone know where they could reach him. Maybe Bill Geary had his insurance business so well organized that he did not even have to think about it.

As he started his car and swung out into the noon traffic, he remembered that he had the other gun to deliver to George Maxwell. He drove the three blocks to Maxwell Motors, parked, again locked his car, and with George Maxwell's rifle in his hand, he went into the salesroom. At the rear was a small office behind frosted glass, next to the parts service counter.

One of the floor salesmen, a young, nice-looking fellow whom Frank did not know, gave him a startled look and Frank said with a straight face, "Did a bear just walk through here?"

"Just went in the men's washroom," the young man said with an equally straight face.

Frank, moving past him, said, "Good Lord, man, it's a she bear. Now you've done it."

Both men grinned.

The door to the office was open and Frank saw George Maxwell sitting at his desk, his coat hanging on the back of the chair. Frank rapped on the door frame and George looked up.

"Brought your artillery back, George," Frank said.

"You didn't have to do that, Frank. I could have picked it up." George rose, took the rifle, and leaned it in the corner behind his desk. "How are the tests coming?"

"Oh, two or three fellows drop in every day. I take their guns to the sand pit, dig out the bullets, and send them on to Washington. No returns yet."

"How long does it take to hear, Frank?"

"Ten days to two weeks. But if I really have something urgent, I send it to a special department. They'll wire back in two or three days."

"What do you mean by urgent?" George asked curiously. Then he added, "Sit down, Frank."

The sheriff eased into the chair facing George's desk, and George sat down too.

"Well, I can only hold a man seventy-two hours on suspicion of murder. They wire me yes or no before the time is up."

George nodded, his round face solemn, and then cleared his throat. "Frank, am I out of line if I ask how you figure this business with the Judge?"

The expression on Cosby's tough face did not alter; it was bland, uncommunicative. "I don't figure it at all, George. I'm hoping these ballistics tests will show something. We have about a dozen more to come in."

"What if these tests don't pan out, Frank?"

The sheriff shrugged. "Then we assume that the killer walked out of the country, I suppose."

George frowned. "Seems hopeless, some-how."

Frank smiled faintly. "I guess a law officer isn't supposed to say so, but it'll seem hopeless to me, too, if these tests draw a blank. It's like a man with no known enemies being shot down on the street at night with no witnesses. Where d'you go from there?"

"Crazy, I guess," George said.

Frank got to his feet, seeming to start for the door, then he halted. "Oh, I've got Bill Geary's rifle in the car. Couldn't find him at home and he wasn't in his office. His girl said he'd left town. Know where he is, George?"

George regarded him during a long moment of silence and then he said. "Does that mean you suspect him?"

"Hell, yes, I suspect him. I suspect you. I suspect everyone who had a gun in that area. If you left town, I'd want to know for where."

George shook his head. "I don't know where Bill's gone, Frank. I've been trying to get hold of him for three days myself."

"Does he travel much in the line of business?"

"Oh, some," George said slowly. "He's got two or three agents working for him down the valley, but he usually cleans that up in a day. Maybe they have a hot prospect for a big policy and Bill will move in to help. Like I say, it's usually one or two days at the most."

Frank considered this information for a moment. "Did he seem worried to you, George?"

"Anything but," George said. "We both got our elk and came home. The Lord knows we were tired, but I don't think either of us was worried." He paused. "Why d'you ask that?"

"Well, Mac seemed to think Bill resented having the serial number of his gun taken down."

George nodded. "He did, but you know Bill. He was still boiling over the divorce settlement." George smiled and added, "I think he's had enough law for a while, Frank. This gun business is sort of the straw that broke the camel's back. Sure he was mad, but he let Mac take the number of his gun."

"True enough," Frank said idly. "Well, I'll be seeing you, George."

"You want Bill to get in touch with you?"

"No, I don't know what I'd say to him, George. So long now."

The sheriff went through the showroom, let himself out, and got into his car. He did not start the engine at once, but sat there, gazing down the street at nothing in particular.

There was something strange in Bill Geary's absence, he thought. Bill's secretary was concerned, and it seemed to Frank that George Maxwell was also concerned. He remembered that only reluctantly had Bill given Mac the serial number of his gun, and he gave it only because he knew the court order would obtain it in the end. There was, as Sam and Jessie had pointed out, a suggestion of guilt in his balkiness, especially if you consider Bill's quarrel with the Lillards. Conceivably, Bill Geary was on the run. He could be anywhere in the country or out of it by the time the ballistics report was finished.

Why, Frank wondered sourly, hadn't he, the sheriff of Grafton County, had sense enough to ask the FBI to give immediate attention on the ballistics test of the slug from Bill's gun and phone back the results? He knew why he hadn't. It was because he wanted to be as fair with Bill as he was with the rest of the hunters suspected. It was his old failing — or virtue, depending on your point of view — of insisting that all men were innocent and entitled to respect until they were proved guilty. *Don't run, Bill. Don't run,* Frank Cosby thought. *Wherever you are, come back.*

V

Mac knew that unless he boosted his number of checks on hunters' licenses, the Regional Office would want to know why he had such a poor showing. Accordingly, he planned to spend the day on the road checking, and he was just as glad to get away from Jessie for a day. It was an appropriate time for him to leave town, he figured. Jessie was almost sullen after his reprimand to her, and perhaps a little absence would make her heart grow fonder, or at least restore her good spirits.

On his checking chore, he could drop by Cy Hartford's, take a look, and confirm Cy's story of the spotlighter. While the Department was more or less helpless to prevent spotlighting, it wanted to know of the number of confirmed instances of illegal shooting.

As Mac swung east up the highway, he looked at the sky, which suggested there might be some weather on the way. This reminded him that the wood he had cut and stacked under a forest service permit the week before had better be moved down before more snow came. Turning off the highway, he headed down the frozen rutted road towards Cy Hartford's ranch, but because he had a full day ahead of him, he did not stop at the house. He continued on past it until he came to a haystack.

When a dozen magpies lifted into the chill morning from beside the stack, their grating voices shrill and angry, Mac knew this was where the spotlighter had killed. He stopped when he saw a furrow in the shallow snow where the carcass had been dragged to the fence. Climbing through the fence, he went up to where the entrails of the carcass lay, a bloody frozen heap. Apparently, the deer had been clumsily butchered, or else it had been gut-shot, and the hay it had been eating was spilled out of its torn stomach to cover the other entrails. Well, this was just another one for his report, but how many went unreported he would never know.

His day was a routine one of patrol and checking licenses. In midafternoon he came down out of the Bear Pass country and stopped at a wayside hamburger stand on the highway for something to eat.

In the late afternoon he pulled into his place and went into the office. He totaled up his number of checks and tossed the notebook in the basket. Looking at his watch, he saw that

Jessie would be home by now and he rang the Morfitt house.

When Jessie answered the phone, Mac said, "Let's go on the town tonight, Jessie. I feel like a steak and a bottle of wine."

"Oh, Mac, mother's got a huge roast in the oven. I've been trying to get you all day to invite you over. Let's go on the town some other night."

"Suits me," Mac said.

"Come over now, and don't dress up. I've some news for you," she added smugly.

"What?"

"Come over and I'll tell you."

Mac drove over to the Morfitts still wearing his uniform. Jessie met him at the door wearing dark gray slacks and a white blouse. She took him by the hand and led him to the sofa, where an end table held a pair of bourbon-and-waters. Handing him one, she said, "I'm studying to be a complete wife."

"That'll fold up the day after we're married," Mac said. "What's this news you're so secretive about?"

Jessie picked up her drink and stood before Mac, smiling at him in a slightly superior way. "The news is that your friend, Bill Geary, has flown the coop. Left town. Vanished."

Mac frowned. "You sure of that?"

"It came straight from the horse's mouth,

147

Mac. Sam has been calling Clyde Lovell — he was Bill's attorney, you know — for a couple of days. He wanted to set up a meeting with Bill and Lola to see if the alimony payments couldn't be reduced. This afternoon Clyde admitted he didn't know where Bill was and none of Bill's friends knew either. Sam called Frank Cosby to check, and Frank knew about it."

"What's Frank done?"

"Everything he could do, short of an all-points alarm. He's had it on the police radio for three days." Seemingly, Jessie could not resist saying what she said next. "This makes your scolding of me and Sam seem a little ridiculous, doesn't it? If Bill Geary wasn't guilty, why should he run?"

"I don't think he's running," Mac said quietly.

Jessie sat down beside him on the sofa, and went on talking. "Frank checked Bill's agents down the valley. They don't know where he is, his office doesn't, Lola doesn't, nobody does."

Mac pulled at his drink. Whatever reasons Bill had for running, he was sure they did not include an attempt to escape arrest for Judge Lillard's murder. With all his faults, Bill Geary was incapable of killing a man in hot or cold blood.

148

"Anybody's got a right to leave town, Jessie."

"Without telling Frank? Without telling his office or his friends? Then why would he choose the time before the ballistics tests were in to leave?"

Mac remembered now Sam's account of the divorce proceedings. Was Bill off gambling somewhere hoping to win a stake toward his alimony payments?

Jessie interrupted his speculations. "Frank said he's been gone five days. Why, he could be in London, Hong Kong, or Australia by now. Why isn't there a law, Mac, that would let Frank hold a murder suspect?"

"Thirty-one of them?" Mac asked dryly. "They're all as much suspect as Bill."

A be-aproned Mrs. Morfitt appeared in the doorway from the kitchen at that moment, and Mac rose.

"Hi, Mac. Glad you could come tonight. Jessie, could you give me a hand a minute?" To Mac she said, "I won't keep her long, but I'm stuck with a cake I can't get out of the pan."

Jessie rose and followed her mother out to the kitchen. Mac continued standing, holding his drink in his hand. Then he moved over to the cold fireplace and automatically put his back to it. Bill could not have been fool enough to run, Mac knew, because he was incapable of murder. If that reasoning was sound, then where had he gone? The why of it was unanswerable at this moment.

There must be better ways of tracking down a man than putting out an emergency call on the police radio, Mac thought, but what were they? It stood to reason that if, as Jessie suggested, Bill had left the country, he would have been far-sighted enough to make reservations with an airline or travel agency. Maybe the best way to find out where Bill had gone was to find out where he had not gone. Check his phone calls? No, Bill's secretary would have caught that. But what if he had called for reservations when the girl was out of the office, or after she went home from work? Or maybe he called from his apartment.

Jessie came back from the kitchen now and Mac put his drink on the mantel.

"Jessie, when you worked for the phone company, how did you handle long-distance calls?"

Jessie halted in the middle of the room. "What a crazy question!" She added, "Apropos of what?"

"Well, if Bill's running, he's running to somewhere, isn't he? Unless he's panicked or is being chased, the normal businessman calls ahead for rooms or plane reservations, or calls to set up appointments and that sort of stuff. Maybe his phone calls could give a clue?"

Jessie looked doubtful. "If he's running, he wouldn't leave that kind of a trail."

"Exactly. And if he isn't running, he would. Does the phone company keep a record?"

"A bullet-proof one," Jessie said. "When you're connected long distance, a toll slip is stamped by a clocking machine immediately. It gives the time of your call and the date. When you hang up, it gets stamped again to time your call. On the back of the toll slip is the person and number you called, at whatever city you reached."

"Can anybody walk in and ask to see these toll slips?"

"Law officers can."

"Me? I'm a deputy sheriff."

"You can always try it, Mac. You will anyway. Now finish your drink and then you can carve the roast."

When Mac got up early the next morning and looked out of the window, it was snowing. As he prepared his breakfast he made his plans for the day. Yesterday he had planned to haul wood today, but Jessie's news of Bill's disappearance had changed that. If Jessie and Sam and the rest of the town believed that Bill had run to avoid what the ballistics tests would show, it was up to him to find Bill.

Still, there was the wood to get in before it could be snowed in. While he ate his breakfast, he mentally ran through a list of names of men he could pay to drive up to his wood camp and haul the cut wood down. Each name that occurred to him was the name of a man who was hunting or who had bagged his game and returned to his job. He tried to remember the men who had already made their kills but who had no regular jobs. Almost immediately he remembered Chuck Daily's elk and deer. He doubted if Chuck had a job, and he was not sure he wanted him anyway. But because he could think of no other name, he settled on Chuck.

When he stepped outside, he saw that an inch of snow had already fallen. He drove his pick-up toward the heart of town, trying to remember where Chuck Daily lived. He knew it was one of the anonymous unpainted shacks down at the riverbottom.

Dropping down the hill behind the courthouse, he cruised slowly between these relics of the pioneer mining days. Most of them, he knew, were occupied by bachelor old-age pensioners who, unable to work, were trying to stretch out their pension dollars.

Chuck Daily's jeep parked on the road

before a mean shack saved Mac from having to inquire. Chuck, he could see, was chopping wood by the side door to his kitchen.

When Mac got out and closed the door to the pick-up, the door's slam coincided with the sharp crack of Chuck's axe splitting a log, so that Chuck, his back to the truck, did not hear it. Mac was unaware of this as he approached Chuck in his quiet woodsman's fashion. He halted and said, "Hi, Chuck."

Chuck, startled, turned, and for a second a look of terror fled across his face.

"What's the matter?" Mac asked.

"You scared me, Mac. I never heard you come up."

"You were making too much racket, I guess. Do you want to work today and tomorrow, Chuck?"

The sly alertness had returned to Chuck's face as he asked, "Doing what?"

"Hauling wood in my truck. Something came up and I can't go, but I want the wood in before the weather hits."

Chuck looked at the sky in the west. "This could be a good one, all right. Sure, where's the wood at?"

Mac told him the location and told him he would leave the keys in the pick-up if Chuck wanted to make an early start. Mac added, "No booze, Chuck. Remember, you're driving state property."

Chuck's gaze slid away and he said in a surly voice, "Nobody ever caught me drinking on the job!"

Mac thought dryly, *Technically you're right. They never caught you.* But he did not voice the thought. Instead, he said, "Stack the stuff inside the garage against the outside wall."

"Okay, Mac. I'll be around as soon as I finish cutting some wood."

Chuck stood and watched Mac drive off. "Damn, damn, damn," he said softly. He turned, went into the house, and walked over to the table, on which stood a near-empty jug of muscatel. He poured himself a glass of it with a shaky hand and gulped it down. He had given himself away again, he knew. When he had turned to see Mac, he was certain that Mac had come either to arrest him or question him. He knew the terror had shown in his face because Mac had asked him what the matter was. Mac had seemed to accept his explanation that he had been startled, but had he really accepted it?

Chuck, because he thought his knees would fail him, sank into a chair. The alcohol warmed his stomach and coursed pleasantly through his veins, but neither his courage nor his confidence returned. Reason argued that if Mac had suspected him he would have asked questions. Maybe Mac wanted to watch him, or maybe this was simply a ruse to get Chuck's fingerprints from the steering wheel of the pick-up. Although it was chilly in the room, Chuck started to sweat. Why had Mac come to him, of all people, to offer work?

Well, why not? He was one of the town's handymen, of which there were all too few nowadays. His visit did not necessarily mean that he suspected anything, and nothing in his conversation had indicated suspicion. *I'm getting spooked*, Chuck thought.

However, there was no denying the fact that he had been scared and that he had shown his fear. Common sense told him that if he acted queer enough and looked guilty enough for long enough, people would begin to wonder why. He resolved then that he would never show fear in the presence of Mac or the sheriff or Sam Lillard. And it was better to be his rude and surly self than to be polite or obsequious. It might even be smart to ask Mac for more work. By the constant testing of himself, he could make himself immune to fear. After all, it was the ballistics test that would prove him innocent. Then what was there to fear?

Half an hour later, Mac heard Chuck pull out in the pick-up. He cleaned up all his correspondence, both official and personal, so he would be free to work on his scheme. Chances were that he would be doing precious little Game and Fish business for the next few days.

It continued to snow and Mac worked on until nine o'clock, when he knew the phone company office opened. Chuck had left his jeep, but Mac wanted to walk. Walking in the snow was something that had delighted him ever since he ran a trap line as a boy. He put on his down jacket and stepped out into the storm. It was going to be a good one, and if it held on long enough with this kind of a fall, the snowplows would be out by noon.

The phone company's office was on the edge of the new business district, almost opposite Bill Geary's office. When Mac entered, stamping the snow from the boots and slamming his hat against his leg to dislodge the snow, he noted that Perry Christian, the young office manager, was at his desk, the rearmost of four lined up in tandem behind the high counter.

When one of the girls came to the counter, Mac asked if he might talk with the manager. The girl indicated the gate at the end of the counter and Mac entered and went toward the manager's desk. Perry, a black-haired young man wearing black horn-rimmed glasses and a proper business suit, was going over a set of

156

figures. When he heard Mac's approach, he looked up and smiled.

"Morning, Mac," he said, standing up. "What're you doing out on a day like this?"

He extended his hand and Mac took it. Mac could never understand why some men, when you come into their place of business, insisted upon shaking hands no matter if you had seen them on the street ten minutes before. It was a facet of public relations that was mildly annoying to him.

"It's a little snowy to be out checking licenses," Mac said. "I can't see twenty feet away in this stuff."

"Well, I guess we've got it coming, and coming," Perry said. "Sit down, Mac. What can I do for you?" Mac sat down in a straight chair by the side of Perry's desk while the manager seated himself again.

"Well, you might help me track down a whopping game violation."

"Can't think how, but we'll try."

Mac had his story ready. "We're trying to track down a poacher, a fellow who shot a cow elk without a permit. We've checked his name against the list of permit holders. On his way out of town he stopped in to say hello to Bill Geary and to make a long-distance call. We know he called home, but we don't know where he lives. We're not even certain about

157

the date he called." Mac paused. "We know his name is Harvey Martin."

"If he was calling his own home," Perry said, "chances are he called collect."

Mac was ready for that one. "No, the first time he called, his youngest child answered the phone. The operator couldn't get her to accept a collect call because she was too young to know what a collect call was. The operator said she'd have to bill Geary's number for the call."

"Didn't the dope ever hear of a person-to-person call?"

"Geary's secretary reminded him of that after he asked the charges and hung up and paid her. You see, Bill wasn't in the office and Martin couldn't wait for him."

"Wouldn't Bill know where he lives?"

"Bill will be out of town for some time, Perry, and we'd like to get on this right away," Mac said. "Could I have a look at Geary's toll slips?"

Perry frowned thoughtfully. "I'm not supposed to make these toll slips public, Mac. Still, this is the same as police business, isn't it?"

"If we can find where this character lives, it'll certainly be court business. He'll very likely draw the maximum fine."

"Just a minute, Mac," Perry said. He rose

and went to the rack of filing cabinets, and from one of them drew out a tray of cards.

He stopped by the vacant desk across from him and laid the file on it. "Trudy's home with a cold, Mac, so you can use her desk. They're in alphabetical and chronological order, Mac. Have a heart and keep them that way."

Mac rose and went over to the empty desk just as Perry's phone rang. He put his pencil and notebook beside the file drawer and lifted out all the toll slips under the heading of "G".

He soon found that Bill had not called a travel bureau or an airline. What he did find out was that, while Bill consistently called his agents down the valley, there was also a number in Jamestown that was called over and over again, both from his apartment and from the agency. None of these calls were person-to-person, so that he had no knowledge of who Bill called, but invariably they were placed around 5:30 P.M. With a sense of disappointment, Mac copied down the Jamestown number and returned the file drawer to its place. Perry was on the phone and Mac made a gesture with thumb and index finger forming a circle that, with his affirmative nod, indicated success.

On his way out he asked the girl at the counter, "Do you have a Jamestown directory, miss?"

"No, sir. It's not in our district," the girl answered.

Mac had his mouth open to ask if the girl could trace the owner of the Jamestown number, when he remembered, or thought he did, that phone companies refused this sort of inquiry. He could probably persuade Perry to get it for him, but he didn't want Perry's curiosity aroused further. He said, "Thanks, anyway," put his jacket and hat on, and stepped out into the storm.

In the half hour he had spent in the office, it had snowed two inches. If this kept up, Mac thought wryly, he would probably have to send a rescue crew for Chuck Daily and the Department pick-up.

Head down against the wind, Mac made his way toward the hotel, a plan already formed in his mind. The persistence of the calls to Jamestown indicated that Bill had a very lively interest there, since they far outnumbered the calls to his agents. He knew that calling the phone company in Jamestown to match the number to a name would draw a firm refusal. However, there was a way out of that. At the hotel, he crossed the tile floor of the old-fashioned lobby to the rank of phone booths and, after consulting his notebook, placed a call to the Jamestown number of Harry Goodwin, the local Wildlife Conservation officer.

When a woman answered, Mac said, "This is Lee McPhail, Mary. How are things with you?" ("Fine. Are you getting this same snow in Ute City?") "Worse, maybe. Mary, is Harry around?" ("He's out checking, like a proper Conservation officer.") "Mary, I've got a Jamestown phone number but I don't know who it belongs to. Could you run through your phone book and track it down for me?" ("You dope. Why don't you call the number and ask who answers?") "I can't work it that way, Mary. Will you hunt the name and street number down and call me back collect in about twenty minutes at my office? You've got the number haven't you?" ("Harry has, but he's got it with him.") Mac gave her his number, thanked her, and hung up.

He walked home in the storm and was shaking the snow off his jacket when the office phone rang. It was Mary Goodwin. "Mac, the phone belongs to Mrs. Vera Sanderson. Eight hundred North Tenth."

"You know her, Mary?"

"This is a small town, Mac, but frankly I've never heard of her."

Mac thanked her and hung up and sat there, his hand still on the phone. If Mrs. Sanderson was listed under that name in the phone book, she was undoubtedly a widow or divorcée. Had Bill been playing around with another woman? If so, it had not come out in the divorce, or Sam would have told him, Mac thought.

On impulse then, he put in a call to Jamestown for Mrs. Sanderson's number. He could hear the phone ringing unendingly, and finally the operator told him the obvious.

Almost thankfully, Mac cradled the phone. If Mrs. Sanderson was Bill's mistress and he asked about Bill, the chances were she would say she'd never heard of Bill Geary. If Bill was there, there was an equally good chance that he would not answer the phone, not wishing to compromise his girl. And if Jessie was right and Bill was on the run, again he would not answer the phone.

Mac got down to work on his monthly report. But he called Mrs. Sanderson every hour, and three times during the noon hour, and never got an answer. Instead of discouraging him, it baffled him. Relying on the phone seemed futile.

He could tell Frank what the toll slips revealed, and Frank would doubtless call the sheriff of Hastings County in Jamestown and ask him to check on Mrs. Sanderson and Bill. Mac knew that if this happened, Bill would never forgive him for embarrassing the two of them. Besides, Frank would hesitate to ask for help from another sheriff if there were no legal grounds for investigating Bill or even checking on his whereabouts.

After trying one more time to reach Mrs. Sanderson and getting no answer, Mac came to his decision. He would go over to Jamestown himself. If Bill was not there, then according to the pattern of toll slips, he would be calling Mrs. Sanderson. If she could be made to understand the importance of contacting Bill, she could give him the information he needed.

He realized suddenly that his pick-up was gone and that he only had Chuck's jeep for transportation. In this storm the drive to Jamestown would be murderous.

Looking at his watch, he saw that Jessie would be back in the office, and he called her to ask if he could borrow her small car. It was parked in front of the office with the keys in it, Jessie said, and he was welcome to it.

The drive to Jamestown was one of the worst Mac could remember. The driving snow of the blizzard hid the road much of the time, so that even with his lights on, he had to stop for minutes on occasion. The drifts in the draws piled up again right after the snowplow pulled through them. Once, in a blinding gust of snow, before he could stop he found that he had nosed Jessie's car into a snowbank in the opposite lane. On the reasonably low pass twenty miles this side of Jamestown, the snow had avalanched in two places and he was stalled along with twenty other cars while a rotary plow cleared a single lane.

It was near four o'clock when he pulled into the outskirts of Jamestown, where the city's plow was doing a valiant job trying to keep the streets open.

Jamestown was a newer town than Ute City, and now its reason for being was its logging industry and its pulp-paper plant. Originally a shipping center for stock, there were only the stone courthouse, the colonnaded brick hotel, and the red-stone bank on a corner to remind it of its origin.

At a gas station, while his tank was being filled. Mac inquired where 800 North Tenth was and he was directed five blocks down and eight blocks to the left.

Mac pulled up at the first house in the 800 block; it was a small, white-painted New England type cottage, but it was snowing so hard that he could not see its number. He stepped out into the blizzard, and was two-thirds of the way up the walk before he could confirm the number. He noted that there were two sets of wind-drifted tracks leading up to the house. With quiet exultation, Mac thought that at least someone with whom he could talk

164

was in the house. He mounted the steps and punched the bell, and after seconds he dimly heard footsteps behind the half-glassed door.

The door opened to reveal a boy about ten years old, who said "Hello" in a faintly puzzled voice.

Mac saw a handsome, broad-shouldered, black-haired youngster who was a miniature Bill Geary.

VI

"Hello, son," Mac said, when he had recovered his composure. "Is Mrs. Sanderson home?"

"No, sir. She's working," the boy said. "She gets off at four-thirty, though."

Mac pushed up his jacket sleeve to look at his wristwatch and saw that it was four-twenty.

"Mind if I wait for her?"

The boy did not answer immediately, but then he asked, "What kind of a uniform is that, mister?"

"Game and Fish Department."

"Has mother done anything?"

"Lord, no," Mac said, and smiled at the boy. "I'm just checking out a car registration. I must have got it wrong, but your mother can put me right."

"Come in," the boy said, and held the door wide.

As Mac was about to step through the doorway he heard footsteps, and then through the door to the left a man appeared.

It was Bill Geary.

Bill hauled up, and for a stunned moment he looked at Mac as if he could not believe his own eyes.

"Hello, Bill," Mac said quietly.

"Mac! What are you doing here?"

"Get me out of the weather and I'll tell you."

Bill said lightly, "Come in." He gestured to the door of the room he had just left and Mac stepped past the boy and entered the room. He heard Bill say, "Better get back to that model, Billy. It's homework after supper, you know." There was an odd gentleness in his voice that Mac did not miss.

He heard the boy go down the hall and climb the stairs before Bill stepped into this pleasant room. There was a fire going in the fireplace on the opposite wall. A thick, solid color maroon rug lay wall to wall under three slip-covered easy chairs and a sofa. A big Matisse print hung over the fireplace, and the back wall held a long, low, well-filled book-case. All this Mac saw in a brief glance before he turned to look at Bill, who was standing just inside the doorway.

"I don't know how you found me, Mac, but you did. Why?" As an afterthought, he said, "Sit down."

Mac took one of the chairs and Bill eased

into the one opposite. Mac said, "Bill are you running?"

Bill scowled. "From what?"

"From what the ballistics tests on your rifle will show."

Bill's facial expression changed from blankness to near anger. "Why, hell no! Did you come over here to ask me that?"

"I guess I did," Mac said. "Frank's had an emergency call for you on the police radio for three days. I've been trying to get this number all day."

Bill looked puzzled. "There's been nobody home until an hour ago. Is this about the ballistics test?"

Mac felt a sudden and overwhelming relief. This was not the reaction of a man who had run from a knowledge of guilt, "You stupid Mick!" Mac said in a half-scolding tone. "Don't you realize that along with thirty other guys you're suspected of Judge Lillard's murder? A lot of people, including Frank, think you're hiding. You didn't tell your office or your friends where you were going. Some people have you placed in Australia or Europe. Why didn't you tell Frank where you were going?"

Bill shrugged, and then smiled. "Oh, I forgot to, Mac. I had a far more important thing on my mind than calling Frank."

"Like what?"

"Getting married and going on a wedding trip."

For a moment Mac did not know if he had heard right. Then he came up to Bill, held out his hand, and said, "Congratulations, Bill."

"When you meet my wife, you'll know I deserve them, Mac." He added, "The least I can do for you after that drive is offer you a drink. What'll you have?"

Mac told him bourbon and water, and Bill moved over to the portable bar near the door. Mac sat down again, trying to make sense of what he had seen and heard in the last few minutes. Billy was Geary's son, probably by a previous marriage. But in all the years that Mac had known and been associated with Bill, there had been no mention of it. It was not a thing a man would be ashamed of, so why had he kept it a secret?

Bill, a drink in each hand, walked over to Mac and gave him his glass. Mac lifted it in toast. "All kinds of luck to your new marriage, Bill."

"Thanks. I won't need it, but I like the sentiment, Mac."

They both took a pull on their drinks, and then Mac said, "I never knew you'd been married before you were married to Lola, Bill."

Bill's glance was level and friendly. "I wasn't."

169

Mac frowned. "But the boy's yours. There's no mistaking it."

Bill said soberly, "Didn't anyone ever tell you that you can acquire a son without being married to his mother?"

When Mac fully understood the meaning of what Bill had said, he felt a wretched embarrassment. "Oh, hell, Bill. I'm sorry."

"For what? You asked the question everyone in Ute City would ask. That's why I'm selling my business and moving here." Bill walked up to the fireplace and stood with his back to it while Mac remained silent. Then Bill asked, "What would the kids in Ute City say when Billy showed up with me? What would everybody say? They'd think the boy grew up in a hell of a hurry, wouldn't they?" He paused. "Here, our story is already accepted. People think that eleven years ago Vera and I were married, and were divorced a year later. The story is that she remarried and her husband died. Now that I'm divorced, we got remarried. I can make that story stick in Jamestown, Mac, but in Ute City I can't. Lola would see to that."

"Where does the Mrs. Sanderson come in?" Mac asked, still puzzled.

"It came out of a phone book, Mac. A girl with a baby should be a Mrs., and it's simple enough to move to a new place with a new

170

name." He paused, then said, "Remember what I was ten years ago, Mac?"

"You were pretty hairy, as I recall it."

"So hairy that Vera wouldn't marry me," Bill said. "She chose the illegitimate baby and the new home over living with me as my wife, and I can't say I blame her. Now we have a chance to make up for the ten years we missed together." Bill grinned. "This story has a happy ending, Mac. Now that you know it, pretend I never told you."

Mac smiled. "I haven't heard a word you said."

There was the sound out on the porch of someone stamping snow off their boots. Then the door opened and a woman stepped into the room. At the sight of Mac she halted, and Mac rose.

"Vera, this is my old friend, Lee McPhail. I've talked to you about him many a long hour." He turned to Mac. "The new Mrs. Geary, Mac."

Vera Geary advanced, extending her hand, and Mac took it, bowing slightly. She was a handsome woman, rather than a pretty one. Her chestnut hair was still powdered with snowflakes. She had a short nose under grave dark eyes, and Mac had the feeling her pleasant smile had been something of a rarity in the past. She slipped off her coat, moved over to

Bill and kissed him, and Mac saw that she had a trim young figure.

Mac said, "I wish you all the happiness in the world, Mrs. Geary. I warn you, though, you've married a character."

Vera Geary laughed. "Every woman does."

Mac lifted his glass. "Here's luck to you both."

While Bill made Vera a drink, she chatted with Mac, mostly about the unseasonable storm. She was, Mac thought, a pleasant sensible woman, quietly gay and obviously happy.

Mac finished his drink quickly and then said, "I better be shoving off while there's still daylight."

"I don't envy you your trip," Vera said.

Mac shrugged. "That's the high cost of living in the mountains, Mrs. Geary." To Bill he said, "Give Frank a ring, won't you, Bill?"

"Right away," Bill said. "In a way I'm sorry you had to come over, Mac. But in another I'm glad you did. You can see I'm in safe hands."

Mac shook hands with them both, thanked them for the drink, and was ushered out by Bill.

It was still snowing, but Mac thought it was slacking off a little. Once in Jessie's car, headed home, he began to reflect on Bill's

172

strange but very human story. He thought he knew now that Bill's story to the court of his gambling losses was simply a coverup. The missing money had gone for the support of a son and his mother. And for the first time he suspected Lola Geary, without knowing it, had done Bill Geary the greatest favor he would ever receive.

After unloading and stacking his second load of Mac's wood by the light of his jeep's headlights, Chuck backed the pick-up into the garage, climbed into his jeep, and headed for town. It had been one wild day working in the storm, Chuck thought, and he figured he had earned the right to a couple of shots of whisky.

Driving downtown, he noted that the snow-plows were still working after dark, trying to keep ahead of the still falling snow. Chuck pulled up by the Elite and went into the grimy bar. It was almost deserted at this hour, for the winos, along with other customers, were at supper. Mike Conti was behind the bar, and when he saw Chuck he began to reach for the muscatel. Chuck bellied up to the bar and said, "Whisky this time, Mike."

Mike poured a shot of whisky in a shot glass and said, "Some snow, huh? This is January stuff."

"Yeah. The plows are still working up in

the east end of town."

"You can damn well bet they aren't working our road, Chuck. We get plowed last every time," Mike said sourly.

Chuck poured the gullet-tearing whisky down his throat, caught his breath, and said, "Yeah, we get no grading in the summer or plowing in the winter. We're poor people."

Mike laughed grimly. "You can always tell the poor people, Chuck. They live down in the riverbottom and have the best vegetable gardens. Me, I like it down there, even if they forget we've got a road."

Chuck took a second shot and paid up, then he went out to his jeep and headed home. Sure enough, the road had not been plowed. He backed into what passed for his front yard, so that if the plow came by in the night he would be headed right for bucking the drifts it would leave behind it.

Once he had the fire started, Chuck poured his customary glass of muscatel and sipped it while cooking up a mess of ham and eggs. This he was eating out of the skillet when he heard a knock on the door. *That damn Minnie,* he thought, and yelled, "Come in."

He heard Minnie stomping the snow from her galoshes, then the door opened and she stepped inside. She was wearing a man's worn jacket three sizes too big for her over her bulky sweater, and she was carrying something wrapped in a clean towel. Snow powdered her frowzy hair and her raddled face was red with the cold.

"I baked this afternoon, Chuck. Thought you'd like some bread." She went over to the table and laid the bread on it.

"Much obliged," Chuck said, with his mouth full of egg. He gestured with his fork to the wine. "Help yourself, Minnie."

Minnie poured herself a glass of wine and moved over to Chuck's cot and sat on it.

"I'll bring you over a piece of meat, Minnie, soon as I get around to it."

"I'd like that," Minnie said.

Suddenly she lifted her head, sniffing. "Aren't you getting sick of the smell of that gun oil, Chuck? It's a good enough smell, but I couldn't sleep with it."

"I'm used to it."

Apparently her mention of gun oil reminded Minnie of something else and she looked in the corner where Chuck's guns were stacked. "Why is Frank Cosby keeping your thirty-ought-six, Chuck?"

Chuck's fork stopped halfway to his mouth as he looked at Minnie. He had forgotten she knew about his 30.06, and now the old panic that he thought he had conquered returned.

"Why, to test it, same as everybody else's,"

he managed to get out.

"It was a thirty-ought-six that killed the Judge, you know."

Chuck put down his fork full of food and shoved the skillet away from him. Suddenly he was no longer hungry. He cursed himself bitterly for pretending Frank still had his rifle. Why hadn't he told her it was in the shed? It was too late now.

"All the other rifles have been returned," Minnie said, and asked again, "Why d'you suppose he's keeping yours, Chuck?"

"Who said they'd been returned?" Chuck asked.

"I iron for Harve Wallis." Minnie frowned. "Harve will be by to pick up the ironing tomorrow. I'll ask him."

Chuck's panic was compounded. If Minnie asked why his rifle was being held, Harve would tell her that he had already turned the rifle back, as he had done a couple of days after Chuck got back from his hunting camp. Sure as hell Minnie's question would be dynamite, and sure as hell Minnie would name the caliber of the rifle to Harve. He knew Minnie well enough to foretell exactly what would happen when Harve said the rifle had been returned. Minnie would say she had Chuck Daily's word that it had not. This would make Harve suspicious enough to report it to

Frank, who would question Minnie and then himself. Once Frank said that the 270 had been returned, Minnie would correct him, saying that it was the 30.06 she was talking about, not the 270.

Chuck reached out and refilled his glass. The neck of the bottle in his trembling hands beat a tattoo on the glass's rim. *You're dead*, he told himself. *If Cosby talks to her, you're dead.* He knew he could not get her drunk enough so she would not remember this conversation; too many drinking bouts with her had shown him she had total recall up until the time she passed out. If he told her to forget about Harve Wallis, and that he would pick up the rifle tomorrow, she would be at him about it again until she became suspicious because he could not show it; and even if he could still her temporarily, she and she alone knew about his 30.06. He could not extract promises from her not to talk to Harve Wallis, nor could he threaten her, for she would guess immediately that he was trying to hide something. She was holding his life in the palm of her hand and did not even know it.

The thought was intolerable to Chuck. It not only frightened him but infuriated him, and now he looked at Minnie with the purest hatred. The thought crossed his mind that he could marry her — hadn't he heard that a wife couldn't testify against her husband? — but even that would not help, for when the occasion for testimony arose, it would be too late.

"Can I have a little bit more, Chuck?" Minnie asked.

"Go ahead," Chuck said dully. *Get rid of her*, he thought. *It's her life or yours.* But how, he wondered. He had got away with it once, but this time there would be a body to dispose of.

Suddenly, his mind racing just ahead of panic, he remembered Mac's wood camp. One of the hundreds of old abandoned mines and prospect holes that were scattered through these mountains was close to where Chuck had cut his wood. Unlike the shafts close to town, this one had not been covered to protect the roaming children of the community. Yesterday, after he had finished his noon sandwich, he had gone over to the shaft and, out of curiosity, tossed a piece of wood down it. He had listened, but he never heard the wood hit bottom. . . . The wood road was open, and this snow or the next would close it for the winter.

It's you or her, he thought again, as Minnie walked back to the cot. He had come to his grey decision. Rising, he took the skillet over to the rusty sink, which was filled with greasy pans and graniteware. Minnie heard the clatter in the sink when Chuck put down the skillet and she got up and came over.

"No wonder you've got to eat out of a skillet," she said in a scolding tone. "Every dish in your place is dirty."

"I still eat, though."

Minnie took the kettle from the back of the stove, filled it with water and put it on the front of the stove. Chuck lifted a lid and stuffed the stove with wood. He was searching his mind for the easiest way to do this. A shot could be heard and remembered, and would also necessitate some cleaning up.

Suddenly he looked at the heavy piece of wood in his hand and then at Minnie. She was stacking the dishes on the counter beside the sink, her back to the table. Silently Chuck, hiding the length of wood against his leg, walked over to the table behind her.

"Don't you have any soap?" Minnie asked, not looking around.

"It slipped out of my hands tonight," Chuck said. "It's under the sink."

Minnie leaned down to look. Chuck raised the piece of wood and brought it crashing down on her skull. Minnie simply folded onto her knees and then onto her face, and lay motionless.

Chuck put the wood down and rolled Minnie over on her back and saw that she was unconscious. He straddled her, put both hands around her neck and choked her, both thumbs pressing against her windpipe. Her body protested faintly but there was no volition behind it. He held on until his arms ached, and then he leaned down to see if she was breathing. She was dead.

Chuck stood up, took a heavy sweater from the wall and put it on, and put his jacket on over it. Taking his cap from its nail, he stepped outside and went over to his jeep. As he started it, he noted that the tank was almost full and then he backed the jeep around to the door. He entered the house and blew out the lamp on the table, then he dragged Minnie across the room to the doorsill. A car was coming and he waited until it was past, then he lifted Minnie and dumped her body in the back of the jeep. Her legs stuck out, and he had to bend them to wedge her in. Afterwards he went back into the house, picked up Minnie's jacket from the chair, and stripped the blanket from his cot. He came out and locked the door behind him. Then he remembered her galoshes. Entering the house again, he found them and wedged them under her arms. He covered Minnie's body with the blanket, tucking it around her so it would not blow off.

It was snowing lightly as he pulled onto the

road and headed east. He met few cars on the highway, and after turning off the road that passed Harbor's ranch he met none. Finally, he came to the wood road. Only then did he remember that his jeep was narrower then Mac's truck and that he could not use the ruts. However, with the jeep in low, low, and one set of wheels in the rut, he crawled up the mountain until he came to the camp.

He drove as close to the shaft as he could and got out, leaving his headlights on. He lifted Minnie out and carefully made his way through the snow down the sloping pile of tailings until he was as close to the shaft as he dared go. Then, with a tremendous heave, he hurled Minnie's body towards the shaft. It landed on the lip of the shaft, and then rolled over and disappeared.

Her body must have hit the rotten cribbing and torn some of it away, for he heard the sound of wood splitting. As with the piece of wood he had thrown down the shaft earlier, he did not hear her body hit bottom. Of course, the galoshes that followed made no sound whatsoever.

When Mac stepped out of his back door next morning, the sun on the new snow was so dazzling he almost winced. It was cold and clear, and every roof in sight held its ten-inch burden of new snow. He noted the two sets of tracks in the drive, one from Chuck's jeep, which was undoubtedly parked in the garage, the other from his own pick-up which Chuck had taken for the second day of wood-hauling. Mac had been tired from the drive last night and he had slept so soundly that Chuck's early departure with the pick-up hadn't even wakened him.

He entered his office and built a fire; then he went into the garage, which held Chuck's jeep, took down the snow shovel from its nail in the back wall, and spent the next half-hour shoveling a path from the back door to the office and from the front door to the street.

Afterwards he returned to his office and sat down before the typewriter. In his basket was a petition with fifty-odd signatures of townspeople and ranchers asking that seven miles of the Ute River above the town be closed next season except for fly-fishing. Judge Lillard's signature headed the petition. Looking at it, Mac felt a swift sadness. The Judge had held an abiding contempt for bait and hardware fishermen, maintaining that with the modern spinning rods and artificial lures, a six-year-old boy could kill more fish than a fly fisherman of thirty years' standing, and still never experience the true thrill of the sport. Well, the Judge would never hook another rainbow on his favorite Adams, but perhaps his name would lend weight and prestige to the petition.

Mac was halfway through the covering letter that would go to the Department with the petition, when his phone rang. It was Frank Cosby asking him if he could come down to the sheriff's office. Unaccountably, Frank's voice sounded both angry and listless, and after Mac hung up he wondered what was troubling him. Mac quickly finished his letter, signed it, put it in an envelope along with the petition, and went out to Chuck's jeep. Chuck had, for some unknown reason, taken the keys, and Mac was almost glad he had. He welcomed the walk this beautiful morning.

He mailed the letter in the street box close to Lillard's office, and cut across the park to the courthouse. New snow lay bright around the park and on the trees. The benches in the center of the park appeared to be upholstered with white pillows. The stone soldier in the courthouse yard had acquired a new cape around his shoulders, as well as a comical addition to his flat cap.

When Mac reached the sheriff's office he paused in the doorway. Frank, head down, was pacing the area behind the counter like a caged animal; after watching him a moment, Mac stepped in. Frank looked up at his entrance, then went over to his desk, picked up a letter, and tossed it on the counter. "It's all in there. We drew a blank on all our ballistics tests. Those last five reports make thirty-one negatives."

Mac read the letter and threw it back on Frank's desk, feeling an overwhelming gloom.

"That takes Geary off the hook," Frank said. "But it leaves me on. Oh, he called me last night from Jamestown."

Mac stood motionless for a moment, letting this appalling news sink in. In spite of Jessie's doubts, Mac, like Frank, had clung to the hope that the ballistics tests would turn up the murderer. He said, "Does Sam know?"

Frank nodded. "I called him and told him. D'you know what he came back with? He's putting twenty-five hundred dollars in escrow in the bank today to be used as a reward for information leading to the conviction of his father's killer."

"You sound mad."

"Why the hell shouldn't I?" Frank said. "It's a reflection on me and all I've done."

Mac shook his head. "That's not true, Frank. You know the county can't put up any reward money. You also know that a money reward is going to make a lot of hunters remember things they wouldn't have otherwise. Also, if we have a couple of bums hiding a secret, that money is an easy way to pry apart their friendship."

"Maybe," was Frank's laconic answer.

Mac shrugged. "So we missed, Frank, but we tried."

Frank said angrily, "I don't think we did miss, Mac. I think if you damn deputies could all remember exactly what happened with each of you on the day you questioned those hunters, we'd have a hint."

Mac halted. "All of them gave us their serial numbers and brought in their guns. What more could we tell you?"

Frank said, still angry, "Don't ride me today, boy. I'll eat you alive."

"I'm sorry, Frank. I know I've told you everything that happened that day."

Frank walked to the window, scratching his red hair as if he were trying to rub an idea into his head. He turned then and said, "I know you did, Mac, but I want it in writing."

Mac frowned. "In writing?" he echoed.

Frank's voice was harsh now as he said, "Look, I listened to five stories from my deputies. I think I know what they said, but I don't know what they saw. Maybe one of those hunters had two rifles. Maybe we missed a hunter. Maybe one of my deputies said he checked every person in camp when he didn't. I think someone is sitting on something and they don't know it, Mac."

Mac said dryly, "This is the first time I've seen you wish instead of think, Frank."

Frank said sharply, "All right, *you* think then."

"I think somebody walked through that country, killed the Judge, and walked out."

"If that's so, we might as well quit, and I don't quit. I'm doing the only thing I know with what I have, and, by God, my deputies are going to help me!"

He began to pace again and Mac said nothing. He could understand Frank's agony of frustration, and he had to concede that probably Frank was doing the only thing he could.

Frank said then, "I called Jessie before you came. Sam's tied up until three this afternoon. I made a date for you. She'll take your deposition and Sam's and type them up for me. As soon as Harve gets back, I'm going out this afternoon to round up the rest of the deputies and bring them in to Jessie."

The phone rang at that moment and Frank moved over and lifted the receiver.

"Sheriff's office," he said, and waited a moment. "Talk louder, Hutch, I can't hear you." He paused to listen. "Yes, they're all in, Hutch. None of the rifles was the one that killed the Judge." . . . "I know, Hutch, but I'm not quitting." . . . "Yes, so long, Hutch."

186

He hung up. "He's called twice a day for the last five days."

Mac moved over to the counter and picked up his hat. "Frank, have you phoned the wire services about the tests and the reward money?"

"Why? I look enough like a monkey now."

"Quit feeling sorry for yourself," Mac said angrily. "If Sam's reward has any hope of turning up information, it ought to get the widest kind of publicity."

Frank pondered this a moment and again he walked to the window. Presently he turned and said, "You're right, it should. I'll call old Harridge at the *News* and he'll phone them."

By 11:30, the chain reaction which had been started by Cosby's call to Harridge was in motion. The wire services in Granite Junction came back at Frank on the phone. The reward offered and the failure of the ballistics tests to pin-point the gun of the killer reawakened the Judge Lillard murder story.

He was still talking when Selena appeared in the doorway to announce that their noon meal was ready. She pointed downstairs and Frank, still on the phone, nodded. When he had finished, he hung up and was starting for the door when the phone rang again. He was sure the call would be from another reporter and he was hungry. They could try again after he had eaten.

Down in the apartment, Selena already had his and Harve's food dished out and was seated waiting for them. As Frank came into the kitchen he said, "Harve won't be here. He's out in the country, checking a stock theft."

"Shall I put his plate in the oven?"

"No. He'll be gone most of the afternoon."

He sat down and they both began to eat. Selena had been married to Frank long enough to sense his mood, and she knew that at the moment it was vile. A more mature and a more perceptive woman would have ignored his mood, or else would have tried to cajole him out of it, but not Selena. She attacked like a barracuda.

"What you sore about?" she demanded. "What's wrong with the food?"

He held a fork full of food halfway to his mouth and looked at her. Her hair was in curlers, with not even a scarf to hide it, and for the thousandth time Frank wondered why a woman who presumably curled her hair to make herself attractive to men would let herself be seen in such an outlandish get up.

"The food's good." he said. "It's just that I heard bad news from Washington today." He paused. "We got negative reports on all the ballistics tests."

"You mean you went through all that hokus-pokus for nothing?"

"It's possible," he conceded. "We're re-checking on the hunters' stories." He added, "Sam Lillard has offered twenty-five hundred dollars' reward. Maybe that'll turn up some information we're lacking."

"Twenty-five hundred!" Selena exclaimed, and then said immediately, "Oh, Frank, you've got to win it!"

Frank's voice was dry as he answered, "You don't win a reward, you earn it. Besides, if I earned it, I wouldn't take it."

He put the forkful of food in his mouth, while Selena put her fork down very carefully on her plate, her eyes alert and watchful.

"What d'you mean, you wouldn't take it?"

"Why d'you think I'm paid a salary if it isn't to hunt down criminals? D'you think I'd work any harder on this case if I knew I'd get twenty-five hundred dollars for tracking down the killer?"

"Well, wouldn't you?" Selena demanded. "That's a lot of money, Frank."

He sighed, shuddered, and put down his fork. He pushed his plate away, put his elbows on the table, and looked at his wife. "You don't understand, do you?" he said, almost gently.

"I understand twenty-five hundred dollars," Selena answered sharply.

"That you do," Frank said. "But what you don't understand is why I won't take it if I earn it. Can't you get it through that bubble head of yours that it's my job to find the Judge's killer. I can't work on it any harder than I have worked, and will work."

"But somebody'll get it," Selena protested harshly. "Why shouldn't it be us?"

Frank leaned forward. "Listen carefully. The Judge's killer will be caught if it takes the rest of my life to catch him. That's the job I'm paid to do and I'll do it, and after I do it Sam's money will stay in the bank. Have you got that straight?"

Selena rose so abruptly that she upset her plate.

"You fool! You think Harve wouldn't take it! No, he's smart! You can't mean what you're saying. If you do mean it, you're crazy!"

"I may be crazy, baby, but that's the way it is."

It was in the middle of the afternoon that Selena, while watching a soppy serial on TV, got the idea. In the serial, the heroine, Gloria, married to a skunk just like Frank, had, after a violent quarrel with her husband, decided to pack up and go home to mother. It was exactly her own situation, and she cried more than a few tears of self-pity. It came to her later, during the commercial following the serial, that besides having a heel and a fool for a husband, she, like Gloria, also had a mother to go back to. She could play in real life the role she had just witnessed on the TV screen. Her mind was made up at that moment.

Turning the TV louder so she could hear it in the bedroom, she went in, took down her suitcase, and began packing. She wondered how she would break the news to Frank. Well, how had the TV heroine broken it to her monster husband? Because Gloria was afraid her husband would beat her, she waited until he was at work, then wrote a note and taped it to the bathroom mirror. Selena was not afraid Frank would beat her, but telling him surely would be the most unpleasant of their many unpleasant scenes. So it would be a note then.

She finished her packing, changed her dress, then sat down at the kitchen table with pencil and paper and wrote her farewell note to Frank. It read thus:

I won't even say dear Frank. I'm leaving you, you beest. I've given the best years of my life to you, little knowing that I was marrying a fool. You are a fool, you know. I can't stand your bullying any

191

longer. Our marriage was fated to fail. I hold no gruge but I simply can't go on any longer. I'm going home to the folks. Goodbye for ever.

She made a point of signing it "Selena Graham," instead of "Selena" or "Selena Cosby."

She slipped the note in the dresser drawer, then called her mother, intending to ask that her father be told to call for her this afternoon at the side entrance to the courthouse. However, the phone rang and rang, and while she heard three receivers lifted on the party line and in one case heard a baby crying in the background, her mother did not answer. Well, she would try later.

Then Selena left the apartment and climbed the stairs to reconnoiter. She hoped that if she could get her father and he drove in for her, Frank would be out, but it really didn't matter. Frank wouldn't do anything in front of her father.

Moving over to the half-glassed street doors of the courthouse entrance, she scanned the line of cars parked there, some still holding the fall of snow on top and hood. A faint pleasure was mingled with a feeling of apprehension as she saw Harve's car. She must say good-bye to him and he would want to kiss her and she would let him, and this time it would be a kiss he would remember.

She turned and walked down the corridor to the sheriff's office and stepped inside. Harve was by the radio, listening to an exchange of conversations between two State Patrol cars and translating the numbers of their 10-code into some meaning. Selena walked up to the counter where Harve could see her. Immediately he switched off the radio, came up to the counter, and said, "Hullo, honey. Visiting day?" Then he added, "You're looking beautiful."

Selena smiled. "When will Frank be back, Harve?"

"Not for a while. He's out in the country on a stock theft."

Selena knew if she was going to be kissed, it could not be done properly across a two-foot counter, so she said, "Harve, I want to talk with you."

Not waiting for his invitation, she skirted the counter and Harve gallantly indicated a chair beside the desk. But as she turned to sit down, Harve put his arms around her and kissed her roughly. This was not the kiss she expected but it was long, and there would be a good-bye one. Gently she pushed Harve away, saying, "Harve, what if someone walks in here?"

"They'd envy me," Harve said. "Sit down, honey."

Selena sat down, and Harve slacked his big frame into Frank's chair at the desk.

"What d'you want to talk to me about, Selena?"

She was silent for a moment, wondering how to say what she had come to say. She wanted to tell him what she was doing and still leave a veiled invitation for him to call on her at her father's.

Now she said bluntly, "Harve, I'm leaving Frank. I'm leaving this afternoon. I just can't stand it any longer."

Harve's pale eyes held a certain sympathy. "Yeah, I figured you two weren't hitting it off."

"The last straw was yesterday," Selena said, anger coming into her voice. "He told me that even if he caught Judge Lillard's murderer, he wouldn't accept Sam's reward money."

Harve voiced only an uncomprehending "Hunh?"

"He said this was a job he was being paid for, and he wouldn't accept the reward if he won it."

Harve said softly, "Boy, wouldn't I! Wouldn't anybody!"

"That's just it," Selena said. "That was the last straw. I put up with his bossing, his meanness, his grouchiness, and his temper, but when he won't accept money that's rightfully his, that's the end."

If Harve noted that Selena was talking as if Frank had already single-handedly turned up the killer and refused the reward, he was too wise to say so. Instead he said, "How long you two been married, honey?"

"Going on seven months."

Harve nodded wisely. "Well, kid, I think you're doing the wise thing. If it don't work in seven months, it won't work in seven years or seventeen years. Pull out while you're young and still have your good looks."

Selena blushed prettily and nodded.

Harve leaned forward now. "Is it divorce you're planning?"

"It sure is," Selena said firmly. "If he isn't mentally cruel to me, then no man ever was to his wife."

Harve nodded agreement. "He can be tough, all right."

"Oh, you don't know!" Selena exclaimed. "He's a monster."

"In bed?" Harve asked idly.

"Yes, in bed, too. He's a monster!"

"Poor kid," Harve said. "I'll bet you cry yourself to sleep every night."

"Oh, I do," Selena said, and as if to prove it, her eyes glistened with tears.

Harve's voice became gentle and sympathetic. "If you're leaving him, where'll you go, honey?"

"Back to my folks," Selena said miserably.

Harve grimaced and shook his head. "You like your mother?"

The question surprised Selena. If she answered it truthfully, she would say the only reason she married Frank was to get away from her mother, but that would not sound right. Instead, she said. "Why, I don't like her or dislike her. She's just there."

"Don't do it, kid. You'll be buried. She'll likely raise hell about the divorce, and every boy that dates you will be on the make."

"Then what do I do, Harve?" Selena asked. "You tell me I should divorce Frank but that I shouldn't live with my family. What do I do? Where do I go?"

Harve reached over and took both her hands in his.

"Come with me to Texas, honey."

Selena could not hide her astonishment. Her mouth opened and her lips moved wordlessly as she looked at Harve.

"I'm nuts about you, baby," Harve said soberly. "Haven't you seen it? I've been in love with you since I first met you."

"You — you never said anything," Selena whispered.

"How could I? You were married. I ain't a man to wreck a marriage unless somebody wants it wrecked."

Selena nodded in agreement to this logic.

"You've loved me all along?" she asked incredulously.

"Why d'you think I kiss you?" Harve asked. "Because I hate you? No, baby, I'm nuts about you. Don't go home. Come with me."

"But — Harve, I'm still married."

Harve squeezed her hand. "What the hell difference does that make? On our way to Texas we'll slide over into Mexico, get a divorce, get married, and head for the ranch."

"Oh, Harve," Selena said. Now Harve rose, tilted her chin, and kissed her gently, affectionately, but not passionately.

"You're like a little kid," Harve said. "Just warm and helpless. Let me do the thinking for you. What d'you say?"

"Oh, Harve," Selena whispered, her eyes starry. "Will you be good to me? Will you love me?"

"The minute you think I don't love you, you can walk off, like you're walking off on Frank."

"And we can really get a divorce in Mexico?"

"Don't you read about these Hollywood broads? It's simple. Pay a spick JP some money and you're single again. How about it? Will you come with me?"

Selena said shrewdly then, "You say you love me now, Harve, but will you love me when you're ready to go home?"

"I'm ready to go home now," Harve said flatly.

Selena looked surprised. "But you said the other day that you'd stay through Thanksgiving."

"Ah, to hell with that!" Harve said arrogantly. "Who'll keep me here?"

"What'll you tell Frank if we leave" — she hesitated — "now, like you said?"

Harve was lost in thought a minute, and then he snapped his fingers. "Baby, I've got it. When Frank comes in this evening, I'll tell him I got a call from my lawyer at home. If I want to keep my ranch, I've got to appear in court. Court's beginning next week. If I drive night and day I can make it through in time. I'll tell him I've got to quit now and I won't show up for supper."

"But we just can't leave together," Selena said in a tone of uncertainty.

"Look, baby," Harve said. "Tonight I'm due to testify again in JP court. If I can't make it, Frank'll have to go himself. As soon as he's gone, I pull up to the side door, pick you up, and we're off. What about it? Say yes, honey."

"All right," Selena said, a quaver in her voice, and then she smiled. "I'll even be cross because you don't show up for supper."

Harve pulled her to her feet, and Selena got the kiss she had been anticipating.

Now Harve slapped her on the fanny and said, "Frank'll be in any time, baby. Just play it cool. Court's at seven — I'll be at the side door at five after."

At three o'clock Mac entered the Lillard office and found the reception room empty. He barely had a chance to sit down before a man he didn't know came out of the corridor, picked up an overcoat and hat from one of the chairs, and went out. Jessie came out from the corridor then and saw Mac. He came to his feet and moved toward her. In her dark plaid skirt and light green sweater, she seemed too cheerfully dressed for the mood reflected in her face. Mac kissed her and she clung to him for a brief moment.

"Sam told me what Frank wants," Jessie said and added, "Frank also told Sam that Bill Geary called last night."

"I told him to," Mac said. He told of his trip to Jamestown yesterday which had been suggested by his visit to the phone company, and said that Bill, far from running, had been on his wedding trip.

When he was finished, Jessie said, "Well, I guess I'm never right about anything except the man I'm going to marry. Come on back, Mac."

At Mac's and Jessie's entrance into the office, Sam tiredly lifted his hand in greeting. "I've never tasted crow, Mac, but I'll eat it if you say so. I mean about Bill."

"No crow, Sam. You had no reason to love him."

Jessie seated herself in the straight-back chair, while Mac eased into the client's easy chair. She told Sam how Mac had traced down Bill and visited him. Sam's only comment was, "You make a pretty good friend, don't you, Mac?"

Then he straightened up and said, "Down to business. If Frank wants to read a deposition instead of hearing it, I suppose we should be agreeable." He added, "You're not used to dictating, Mac, and I am. Why don't I give it to Jessie and you stop me if I leave out anything?"

At Mac's nod, Sam began to dictate the events of that well-remembered day. He told of their seeing tracks of the jeep that turned off from the wood road and of their plan to ignore them temporarily for the most distant camp. His telling of their encounter with Geary and Maxwell was detailed and accurate. He described the uneventful back-tracking to the jeep tracks, where an older set of tracks was noted. His description of their encounter with Chuck was accurate, and included Chuck's account of hauling out a deer earlier the day before on the arrogant assumption that he would get an elk and that he didn't have room for both in his battered jeep.

"Hold it a minute, Sam," Mac interrupted. "Using our poor hindsight, when d'you think those jeep tracks were made?"

Sam frowned. "They were pretty faint, Mac. I think we both remember Chuck's telling us he was skinning out his buck when it began to snow."

"You really think he got a buck?" Mac asked.

"Well, you're the game warden. Find out."

"I'll do that when we're through. Go ahead, Sam."

Sam gave the details of their routine investigation of the other two camps and finished his account with their return to Mrs. Horn's ranch. When he finished, he asked Jessie to read back the deposition. There were no corrections, and Jessie went out.

"I'd say Frank is in for some pretty dull reading," Sam said.

Mac rose. "Well, it's at his invitation. See you later, Sam."

He was halfway to the door when he remembered something. Halting, he turned to

Sam and said, "I'm afoot, Sam. Chuck Daily's hauling wood in my pick-up and he left me his jeep. The trouble is he took the keys. Can I borrow your car to go check on Chuck's meat?"

Sam reached in his pocket and handed Mac the keys. "It's parked this side of the hotel, Mac."

Mac nodded and went out. As he passed Jessie's desk, she said, "I'll have this for you before five, Mac."

"I don't think there's that much hurry, Jessie. I'll pick it up in the morning." He nodded to an elderly woman sitting on the sofa as he went by her.

After finding Sam's car, a blue Mercedes sedan, Mac headed for Chuck Daily's place, taking the road down the hill behind the courthouse. The snowplow had been through, piling the snow in high banks on either side of the road, blocking driveways and paths not yet shoveled that led to the mean houses. Mac pulled up where a path should have been, climbed the bank, moved up to Chuck's shack, and halted by Chuck's chopping block. Obviously, Chuck had not returned from his wood-hauling. Mac looked at the shed and reasoned that Chuck's meat would be hanging inside, since Chuck could afford neither a deep freeze nor the expense of a locker.

Tramping through the unmarked snow, Mac went up to the double door of the ramshackle shed which undoubtedly in the old days had housed a wagon and stalled a team. There was no lock on the door and Mac yanked at the door, fighting the banked snow until he had space enough to move through the opening and into the shed. A single window showed him the buck hanging from a rafter by its heels and covered by a dirty canvas. The quarters of the elk hung from butcher's hooks nailed to the rafters.

When he went over to the buck, he saw that the head had been severed from its body. Chuck had already cut the tongue from the tagged head as the first reward of the new season's hunting. A nail, used as a pin, held the two ends of the rotted canvas that shrouded the deer and Mac removed it. The carcass had been skinned and the ribs propped open. All in all, it looked like a well-cared-for piece of meat.

Mac looked at the exit bullet hole in the shoulder, but he could find no mark of the bullet's entrance. The buck was probably gut-shot, he thought. He was about to turn away when he saw wisps of something that was pressed by dried blood in the chest cavity. He reached in and pried loose one of the pieces and examined it. It was a stem of alfalfa hay.

Now that's curious, Mac thought. Unless Chuck had traveled a dozen miles to get his buck — and he had said he got it at first light — the deer couldn't have been feeding on alfalfa. A deer shot in the vicinity of Chuck's camp would have the natural grasses and twigs from high-country brush in its stomach.

Mac leaned closer and found more wisps of alfalfa hay sticking to the carcass. It looked as if the carcass had been hastily wiped out with a gunny sack or cloth. He straightened up and stood there, lost in thought. Chuck had been lying about the location of his kill. But why?

Suddenly Mac thought of Cy Hartford's story of the spotlighter. Hadn't Cy said the spotlighter had got his deer the night of the opening day of hunting season? Mac was sure he had, and now he felt a faint excitement stirring in him. Could that spotlighter have been Chuck Daily? Chuck had said he left for town just after it began to snow on opening day. He could have waited in town until nightfall, could have gotten his deer, and could have returned to his mountain camp later that night. Why would a man originally camped in the heart of an excellent deer and elk area leave his camp to spotlight a deer some thirty miles away? It didn't make sense, yet everything pointed to the fact that Chuck had done just that.

Mac pulled out his handkerchief and carefully wrapped the wisps of alfalfa in it, and then pinned back the dirty canvas as he had found it. Afterwards, he back-tracked to Sam's car and drove off. He had a feeling that he was on to something, but just what he didn't know.

It was close to five o'clock when Frank deposited Glenn Hartsell, one of the deputies who had visited three of the hunting camps, at the office of Lillard & Lillard with instructions to give Jessie a detailed deposition. Afterwards he drove around the square, parked, and went into his office.

Harve was there, pacing the floor on the public side of the counter, and Frank, unheard, stood in the doorway a moment, watching and wondering. Harve, who had seen Frank pull in, had waited until he heard his footsteps in the corridor to go into his act. Now, at the end of the room, he turned, started to pace back, and then caught sight of Frank.

"Are you troubled about something, or just exercising?" Frank asked.

Harve came up to him, halted, and said, "Man, am I glad you're here!"

Frank only frowned, puzzled.

"I got a call this afternoon from my lawyer

down in Texas," Harve said soberly. "I got to get down there, Frank, like day before yesterday. The Judge wants me, along with my lawyer, in court Monday. If I drive straight through, I reckon to make it."

"This about the ranch?"

"It sure is," Harve said. "I asked Abe if he couldn't get the Judge to postpone the hearing for a month, but Abe had already asked him and been turned down."

Frank moved over to the counter and tossed his hat on it, then unzipped his jacket. "Sounds like a tough judge."

"They're rigging it, Frank," Harve said earnestly. "You don't know what a Texas county judge can be like. They figured Abe couldn't get in touch with me soon enough for me to be there."

Frank nodded in sympathy as he shucked off his jacket and put it on the counter beside his hat.

"Frank, I hate like hell to quit now, but you can see how it is. Either I make that Monday hearing, or I got no ranch."

"Sure."

"Like I said, if I drive straight through, I can make it. I should have left three hours ago when Abe called, but I wanted to explain it to you."

"I appreciate that, Harve," Frank said.

206

"Now you better get on your horse."

Harve nodded and walked over to the wall hook, where he took down his jacket and Stetson and put both on. Then he came over to Frank. "I hate like hell to run out on you, Frank, but I never expected things to break this quick."

Frank gave him a friendly smile. "Things like that happen, Harve — nothing we can do about it. I'll miss you." He extended his hand and Harve wrung it firmly with his.

"You got some pay coming, Harve, but the commissioners will have to sign a warrant for it at their next meeting. Where do I mail it to you?"

"Rio Medio, Texas. I'll get it." He paused. "Oh, I forgot. I don't think Tucker has had any cattle stolen. That fence wasn't cut, it was busted, likely by the steers moving with the storm. They'll show up."

He paused and said, almost with embarrassment, "You've been a good boss, Frank. I sure hate to run out on you." Then he added, as if remembering his manners, "Will you say good-bye to Mrs. Cosby for me? I tried to see her myself but she wasn't in. Tell her I'll always remember the good food."

"I'll tell her," Frank said. "Now you'd better beat it — and good luck."

"Luck to you, Frank. I'll be seeing you

sometime." Harve walked to the door, gave a friendly wave, and vanished from Frank's sight down the corridor.

Frank picked up his jacket and hat, rounded the counter, and hung both on the wall hook by the gun rack. He was not really sorry to see Harve leave, but it was mighty short notice, he thought. Still, Harve told him when he was hired that sooner or later he would have to leave for Texas, and his departure was only a minor annoyance compared to the big worry.

Seated at his desk, he ran through his mail, then filed the items required. He had just finished when Selena halted in the doorway long enough to say "Supper's ready." Moments later, when Frank walked into the kitchen, Selena had served up three plates and placed them on the table.

Seeing them, Frank said, "Harve won't be here for supper. He's quit and gone."

"Good riddance," Selena said. "Did you know he was going to quit?"

"No. He got a call this afternoon telling him he had to appear in the Texas court Monday. He's driving straight through." Frank sat down as Selena removed the third plate. "He said to tell you good-bye and that he'd always remember your cooking."

Selena said curtly, "He should. He ate enough of it."

They ate in silence, neither having anything to say to the other. It was when Frank was drinking his coffee that he suddenly put down his cup, snapped his fingers, and looked at his watch.

"What's the matter?" Selena asked.

"Harve was due at JP court tonight. I'll have to go in his place." He rose and headed out of the kitchen, and within moments Selena heard the door slam. She sighed with relief, for she had been watching the wall clock behind Frank as its hands crept closer to seven. There was no way she could have reminded Frank of the JP court without arousing his suspicion. Now, at two minutes to seven, on a Thursday night in October, she was finally free of a husband who had never appreciated her, she thought.

She rose now and automatically reached for the plates to tidy up, and then the thought struck her: *Why should I clean up? Let him.*

Smiling almost secretly, she left the table as it was and went into the bedroom. She crossed to the closet, lifted out her bag, and put it in the hall. Then she returned to the living room and turned on the TV. It was only a few minutes before a knock sounded at the door. Selena almost ran to answer it. When she opened it, she saw Harve's hulking body standing there.

"Let's go, honey. You all ready?" Harve's

voice was crisp and businesslike.

"There's my bag, Harve. Let me get my coat," Selena said. She went over and took her coat off its hanger in the hall, and then, for some unaccountable reason, she moved to the living-room doorway and looked carefully at the room. This was the dungeon she was escaping from and she wanted to remember it.

"Come on, honey!" Harve called. "Let's get out of here."

Selena turned and smiled at him. "Just a sec."

She walked across to the TV set and turned it up full volume. The noise was almost unbearable, even for her, and as she turned away from the set heading for the hall, she thought with pleasure: *That will welcome him.*

The hearing in the JP court lasted two dull hours and the judge's gavel was as welcome to Frank as was the recess bell when he was a school kid. Ducking out into the cold night, the first thing he heard was the clarion voice of a TV set. As he walked the half-block toward the courthouse, the noise grew louder, and he felt a wild and unreasoning anger. That was their set, he knew, and Selena had either gone deaf or was out of her mind. He ran the last twenty yards to the basement entrance, opened the side door, and winced at the clamor. He hurried down the corridor, and saw their door was open. He raced through the hall, crossed the living room, and turned off the set. His fury was almost uncontrollable as he shouted, "Selena!"

There was no answer, and he moved swiftly into the bedroom, then into the bathroom. Not finding her, he retraced his steps and went into the kitchen. The light was on, but she was not there. Then his glance shuttled to the kitchen table.

It was not cleared of the supper dishes, Frank saw with slow shock. Suddenly he remembered the open hall door. It was as if she had been called out by some sudden emergency after he had left. Then the appalling thought came to him that maybe she had answered a knock on the door and someone had made her leave — threatened her or kidnaped her. He dismissed the thought immediately; that stuff could happen in a big city, but not here.

Standing motionless in the kitchen doorway, he said to himself, *Get ahold on yourself, boy. Start thinking.* Turning, he went back to the hall and noticed immediately that Selena's coat was gone. That meant what? A kidnaper might or might not allow her time to get her coat. But why the crashing volume of the TV? Was that to cover up her screams and protests? And why the open door? To him that indicated a hurried exit in emergency.

On sudden impulse, he left the apartment and climbed up to the first floor. It was dark and there were no lights in his office. Again on impulse he shouted "Selena!" and listened to the utter quiet that followed.

As he went downstairs again to their apartment, it occurred to him that perhaps she had gone to the movie, but if she had she would not have left the TV roaring and the door open. Entering the apartment, he came to a halt in the living room and regarded it carefully. There was nothing disturbed, no indications of violence or a struggle.

Methodically, then, he began to review the possibilities. If kidnaping was out, if the movie was out, then what remained? Friends had called on her and she had gone with them? That wasn't likely, he knew. Selena had no friends who were likely to call and whom she would join in a night out. But even if she had gone out with someone, why the open door, why the TV set at full blast, why the uncleared table?

Now he moved into the bedroom and looked about him. The twin beds were undisturbed and were made up, for a change. There were no signs of violence here. Slowly, utterly baffled, he moved into the tiny bathroom, hoping something, anything, would give him a clue. His glance fell on the combination glass and toothbrush holder and he noticed with a start of surprise that there was only one toothbrush in the holder — his.

Moving swiftly now, he opened the medicine cabinet, Selena's cosmetic junk, which usually overflowed the cabinet and tumbled out when it was opened, was gone. He wheeled and went into the bedroom and yanked open the closet door. Selena's nightgown, which always hung on the first hook to the left, was gone. So were several dresses that should have been there. His glance lifted to the high shelf in the back of the closet where their meager luggage was stored. Selena's one bag was not there.

He backed out of the closet into the bedroom, slowly lowered himself onto the bed and, elbows on knees, face in hand, tried to add up the facts. Violence was out. No kidnaper would have allowed Selena to do such a thorough job of packing. That meant that she had left of her own accord. But left for where, and without leaving a message of any sort?

Abruptly then, he rose and moved to the telephone on the bed-table between their two beds. Dialing the number of Selena's parents, who he knew would be in bed, he waited out the fifteen rings it took to bring Mrs.

Graham to the phone.

"Mom, this is Frank. Sorry to get you up, but is Selena with you?"

Mrs. Graham's rasping voice, not even dulled by sleep, came back at him. "Why, no, Frank. Was she coming out?"

"I don't know, Mom. She isn't here and I wondered if she was out there. Probably she's over at a girl friend's and forgot to tell me she was going."

"Well, she isn't here, Frank. Why don't you call Kitty Walsh? I know Selena calls her all the time because Kitty takes the TV Guide."

"O.K., Mom. I'll do that. Maybe she's just gone to the movie and forgot to tell me. Sorry I woke you up."

"She'll be home. Don't worry, Frank. Good night."

Gently Frank replaced the receiver. Pack a bag to spend an evening with Kitty Walsh? Hardly. Slowly Frank moved back to the living room and sat down.

Now he painstakingly added up those things of which he was certain. Selena had packed and left in a hurry. She had not gone to her folks and she had no one else to go to. She had no car and no one she could ask for a ride to wherever she was going. She had no money except for household expenses, and that was always overspent.

Abruptly then, Frank remembered Grandma Graham's ruby brooch that Selena prized so highly that she never wore it. That could be pawned for money. He went into the bedroom to see if Selena had packed that. She kept it, he knew, in the left-hand top drawer of her dresser, along with a bushel of junk jewelry. Pulling open the drawer, he saw an unfolded piece of paper with writing on it that hid almost the entire contents of the drawer.

He picked up the note and read it — the note Selena had intended to stick on the bathroom mirror before Harve had changed her mind.

He read the note once and then again, and on the second reading he began to smile.

"You beast," he said aloud, quoting from the note.

Well, now he knew. Selena, bless her larcenous little heart, had walked out on him. But she had not gone to her folks as her note said she would. She had not had the courage to tell him she was leaving, as Harve had.

Harve!

Was it mere coincidence that Harve and Selena left within two hours of each other? He had not seen Harve leave town, and had only his word that he was going to leave in a hurry. Swiftly now, Frank recalled Selena's words when they were quarreling as to whether he should or should not accept the reward money if he found the Judge's killer: *"You think Harve wouldn't take it? No, he's smart!"*

And now he recalled that lately Selena, whenever Harve was present at meals, was always neat and nicely dressed. When Harve was not at meals, it was pincurls, slippers, and lounging robe. Frank began to laugh quietly, not with hysteria but with a deep amusement. Harve and Selena together. There could not be any other explanation of their disappearance within hours of each other. Harve had the car, the money, and, best of all in Selena's eyes, the ranch in Texas.

He gently put down the note on top of the dresser and then his glance lifted to the framed photograph of Selena on the wall above the dresser.

He said aloud, "Thank you, honey."

VII

Chuck Daily finished unloading Mac's pick-up after dark. All day he had worked fifty horizontal yards and who knew how many vertical yards from Minnie Gerber's body. This hadn't bothered him and he felt no sense of guilt. Animals, he thought, sensed nature's true meaning: Kill what you have to, kill when you're made to. The whole meaning of life was existence, and Minnie had threatened his.

When Chuck went to move his jeep out of the garage and replace it with the pick-up, he found the keys missing. For a moment he pondered over their absence, wondering if Mac had thoughtlessly removed them. Then, on a hunch, he reached in his pocket and found the keys for his jeep. With embarrassment, he realized that he had left Mac afoot this day, and he wondered if Mac would chew him out for forgetting to leave the jeep keys. He doubted it, for Mac was a reasonable guy who would forgive a goof.

After exchanging vehicles, Chuck drove down Mac's drive and stopped at the street.

Should he go home, or should he pick up a couple of snorts at the Elite? He elected the latter because he was as tired as he had been last night after his trip with Minnie to the wood camp. Because of this job he was in the money and could afford hard liquor now.

At the Elite he found the barroom empty except for a stranger who was leaning on the bar at its farthest end talking to Mike Conti. As Chuck bellied up to the bar, Mike left his lone customer and came up to serve Chuck. The wet, unlit cigar, which was his badge of identification, was in the corner of his mouth. Without greeting Chuck, he put his left hand on a bottle of muscatel, his right on a bottle of whisky, turned to Chuck, and raised his eyebrows in inquiry.

"Whisky," Chuck said.

Mike poured a shot glass of cheap whisky, put it before Chuck, and folding his fat arms, leaned on the bar. He gave Chuck time enough to down the shot, then asked, "You figuring to law anybody, Chuck?"

Chuck waited until his breath came back. His sly, unshaven face was blank except for the frown, like a quotation mark, between and above his eyes.

"What are you talking about?"

"Well, I was driving to work about four and passed your place. Sam Lillard's car was parked at your house."

Chuck felt a faint stirring of apprehension and he said, "Are you kidding?"

Mike's normally bland face assumed an air of truculence. He removed his cigar which, when wholly revealed, showed a wad of wet masticated tobacco almost the size of a golf ball.

"Why would I kid you?" Mike demanded. "It was Lillard's car. It's the only one like it in town."

Chuck said, "Did you see Sam?"

"Hell, no! I was driving by. There were marks in the snow where he had climbed over the bank. That's all I know."

Chuck's apprehension turned to alarm. "Did you see the license number?"

Mike rammed the cigar back in his mouth. "Why the hell would I look for a license number? I know Lillard's car, same as you do." He paused and regarded Chuck more closely. "You think I'm making this up?"

"No, no," Chuck said hastily. "I got no business with Lillard, that's all. I can't figure why he wanted to see me."

"Forget it," Mike said curtly. "All I know is I seen his car pulled up alongside your place."

Chuck took out the change for his drink, said, "So long, Mike," and went out into the night. Once in his jeep, Chuck did not start it immediately. He sat there, puzzled as to why Sam Lillard would want to see him. He disliked Sam, and Sam disliked him, and they had nothing in common. *Except for one thing,* Chuck thought, and instantly put that thought aside. Sam had no knowledge of what had happened with the Judge, and the ballistics tests were sure to clear Chuck. But why had Sam called at his house? In spite of his certainty that Sam knew nothing, Chuck could not fight down an uneasiness that bordered on fear.

He drove home at a speed that he tried to keep moderate. He parked his jeep alongside the snowbank in front of his house, went up to his door, and let himself in. He first lit his lamp and looked about the room. Everything was as he had left it. Then, because of what was foremost in his mind, he lighted the lantern and went outside, turning toward the chopping block. There was a trampled area there which he had made this morning when he had lugged in wood. Turning to the side area toward the shed, Chuck held the lantern up high and looked at the snow.

When he saw the tracks in the snow leading to and coming from the shed, his heart almost stopped. He had not been to the shed since it snowed, but here were Sam's tracks leading to it. Almost running, Chuck headed for the shed. When he reached it, he saw by the light of the lantern that the snow had been pushed aside by Sam's efforts to open the door enough to let himself in.

Pulling open the door as far as he could, he knifed through, and held his lantern high. The packed dirt floor was so hard that it held no tracks, and Chuck's glance lifted to the barrels in the corner. As far as he could tell, they were just as he had left them the night he buried his gun, but he had to make sure. He crossed to the corner, put the lantern down, and then hauled the key barrel out of the way. The dirt underneath it was undisturbed. Shoving the barrel back in place, he looked all around the shed. The meat was as he left it and nothing seemed to be out of place. *Then why had he come here?* Chuck thought frantically. *He must have had a reason.*

Standing there with his lantern in his hand, Chuck felt a premonition of disaster. Sam Lillard had been twelve feet from the gun that killed his father. What did he know or suspect?

How had Sam Lillard known enough to go to the shed? It had been a sneak visit, timed when he was away at work, and the visit could have had only one purpose, Chuck thought dismally. Someway, somehow, Sam knew about the buried rifle.

Should he dig up the gun and hide it some-where else, he wondered. Upon reflection he knew that he shouldn't. If Sam knew exactly where the rifle was, he would have it already.

Chuck left the shed and went back to the house. He did not bother to light the fire, but walked immediately to the jug of muscatel and poured himself a full glass. Without tak-ing off his jacket or cap, he sat down at the table and began to put his mind to assessing the situation. He was suddenly aware that he was staring at Minnie Gerber's loaf of bread on the table before him. Cursing, he grabbed the bread, crossed the room and opened the door, and heaved the loaf out into the night.

One thing at a time, he thought grimly. Re-turning to his chair, he drank half a glass of muscatel and then folded his arms on the table, pondering.

What to do now? Should he ignore Sam's visit and pretend nothing had happened? If he did, it would only be an invitation for Sam to return. If he returned enough times, he might find what he was after. Chuck remembered then his vow made after his conversation in the Elite that he had reaffirmed after Mac sur-prised him a couple of days ago: *Whatever you do, act natural. Act just the way you did before.*

All right, he thought. *If this business with the Judge hadn't happened and I knew Sam Lillard was snooping around my property, what would I do?* Chuck knew very well what he would do, and now he rose, turned down the lamp, and went out into the night, locking the door behind him. Tomorrow he'd be late for the wood-hauling because he'd have to wait until the stores opened to buy a padlock for the shed. But there was one thing he could do tonight, he thought, as he headed his jeep toward downtown.

When he came to the business district, he stopped at the first gas station and stepped into the booth beside it that held a pay telephone. After looking up Sam Lillard's number, he dialed and waited. It was Sam and not Mrs. Johnson who answered the phone.

Chuck said, "Sam, this is Chuck Daily."

Sam said in a rather distant voice, "How are you, Chuck?"

"Damn mad!" Chuck said flatly. "What were you doing snooping around my place while I was gone today?"

There was a long pause and then Sam said, "What makes you think I was snooping, Chuck?"

"Don't give me that!" Chuck said in a surly voice. "Your car was parked in front of my place and you left tracks in the snow up to my shed."

Sam's voice was almost genial. "Now,

223

what's in your shed that I'd want, Chuck? Is anything missing?"

"Not that I know of," Chuck said. "But if there is, you'll hear from me."

"If I was there I was trespassing, I guess."

"I may be poor, but I know my rights. A lawyer's got no more right to trespass than I have."

"If your property's posted, you're absolutely right," Sam said.

"I'll post it," Chuck said grimly. "You stay off it or you'll be defending yourself in court."

Sam said smoothly, "That would be nice for a change."

"I mean it!"

"I'm sure you do, and I hear you, Chuck. Good night," Sam said, and the receiver clicked.

Since the pick-up was still next to the garage when Mac went out to his office the next morning, he assumed that Chuck Daily, living up to his reputation, had decided he'd worked enough for a while.

Mac worked for an hour on his report to the Regional Office. In totaling up his patrol mileage, he noted that it was a pretty sorry showing compared to other years. This should have been his busiest week of patrolling his district and checking licenses. Instead, it was the poorest report he would turn in this year. He knew that Osborne, the regional director of the Wildlife Conservation Service and his boss, would forgive the report because a murder had been committed in his district and he'd been working on that. He only hoped that the Game and Fish Commissioners would appreciate this.

At nine o'clock, he took the pick-up down to the courthouse, left it there, and crossed the park to Sam's office. Jessie greeted him warmly and even kissed him, and Mac knew that this was his reward for refraining from saying "I told you so" yesterday when Bill Geary had been proven innocent.

"You're making an old maid out of me, Mac. I had to watch three lousy television shows last night because you couldn't come over. Am I losing my looks?"

"Honey, I've been a deputy sheriff instead of a WCO for the last two weeks. If I don't get this report in, they just might tell me to turn in my suit and keep on being a deputy sheriff."

"I know, Mac," Jessie said, and added a little sadly, "Well, now that the case is hopeless, maybe you can get back to work."

"Something may turn up that will start Frank off again."

Jessie's glance held his. "You don't really

think that, do you, Mac?"

Mac said quietly, "I guess not."

Jessie turned and picked up two stapled sets of papers from her desk. "Here's what you and Sam gave me. And here's Bill Overstreet's deposition. Frank brought him in just before we locked up yesterday."

Mac took the papers and said, "See you for lunch."

"Same time, same place," Jessie said.

Mac went out and crossed the snowy park to the courthouse. Frank was at his typewriter when Mac walked in and put the two typed papers on the counter. "Good morning, Frank," Mac said.

"Maybe it's good to you but not to me," Frank growled.

"What's the trouble?"

"Must be a bigger word than trouble for what I've got." He rose and came over to the counter, put both hands on it and regarded Mac with an expressionless face. "At five o'clock yesterday my deputy quit me. At seven o'clock my wife left me. I think they ran off together."

"Selena ran off with Harve? You're kidding, Frank."

"I don't think I am, Mac. Harve claimed he had a call from his lawyer in Rio Medio, Texas, yesterday afternoon. His lawyer told him he had to be in court by Monday. He was planning to drive straight through. Then last night I found Selena gone."

Mac said quietly, "That doesn't mean she's gone with him."

"Doesn't it? I called Rio Medio this morning and got ahold of Harve's lawyer. He didn't call Harve yesterday and the court won't be in session for another month." He paused. "You figure it out."

"I'm sorry, Frank," Mac said.

"I'm not," Frank countered. "I'm only embarrassed."

"Have you got an alert out for them?"

Frank grimaced. "Hell, no! I might get her back." His glance fell on Mac's deposition and he picked it up.

"Sam and I got together on this yesterday, Frank. Read it now, will you?"

Frank glanced up sharply. "You think you may have turned up something?"

"Read it," Mac repeated.

While Frank read the report, Mac studied the Wanted posters on the far wall. Presently, he came around the counter and took a chair next to the desk. A couple of times Frank grunted when something interested him in the report. Finished, he tossed it on the desk. "You and Sam mentioned that Chuck Daily had gone to town with a buck early that morning. I didn't pay any attention to it then, but when it's down on paper, it's different."

"I felt the same way when Sam was dictating it."

"You couldn't tell by the first tracks how old they were, could you, Mac?"

"They were snowed over. They were just depressions in the snow." Now Mac reached in his shirt pocket, brought out his handkerchief, carefully unwrapped it to reveal the wisps of the alfalfa hay, and laid it on the desk. "What are those, Frank?" he asked.

Frank leaned over and peered at the wisps of hay, picked one up, and studied it. "Why, it looks to me like hay covered with dried blood."

Mac nodded. "Yesterday, when Sam was dictating that deposition, I wanted to know if we could really be sure that Chuck got a buck. Yesterday Chuck was out hauling wood for me, so I went over to his place and looked in his shed. There was a buck all right. He'd been gut-shot and those pieces of hay were stuck to the side of the rib cage. That mean anything to you?"

Frank scowled. "Should it?"

"Chuck said he got the buck at first light. That means he got it close to his camp. But, Frank, there's no alfalfa hay within ten miles of Chuck's camp. If he'd got the buck up there, the stomach should have held bitter bush or wild grasses or willow twigs, but not alfalfa — not unless the buck walked ten miles during the night, and that's not very likely."

Frank studied him in silence. "What you're saying is you don't think Chuck got his buck up in the Officer's Creek country?"

"That's right, and I'll tell you why I don't," Mac said. Then he told of his meeting with Cy Hartford, who had ribbed him about the spotlighting that was going on undetected on his ranch. Mac finished by saying, "The night of opening day a deer was spotlighted and killed at one of Cy's stacks."

"I can see it coming." Frank said sourly. "You think Chuck spotlighted a deer at Cy's."

"Well?" Mac asked.

"I don't believe in coincidences."

"But you grant the deer was eating hay?"

Frank said skeptically, "If you say so."

"Then how does it make sense for a man to leave the country that's swarming with game to kill a deer in low country, and then come back to his original camp in the high country?"

Frank stood up, put both hands in his hip pockets, and walked over to the window, where he stood looking out.

"It doesn't make any sense," he growled.

There was a sound of footsteps in the corridor and both men looked at the door as Sam Lillard entered the room. His overcoat was opened and his dark hat rode at a dead level above his forehead. Somehow it gave him a look of stubborn, uncompromising gravity which his warm smile belied.

"Spotted your truck out front, Mac. How are you, Frank?"

"Just breathing, Sam."

Sam came to the counter and leaned on it, regarding Mac. "I've got a bone to pick with you, my lad," he said, in mock seriousness. "I got a phone call last night."

"So did I," Mac countered. "Three of them. What's so special about a phone call?"

"This was from Chuck Daily." At the mention of Chuck's name, Frank left the window and came up to the counter beside Sam. "Apparently my car that you borrowed was spotted by someone who told Chuck about it. I guess you weren't seen, because Chuck thought I'd driven it. He claimed I was snooping around his place and told me to stay the hell away from it from now on. He even threatened me with a lawsuit if I trespassed again. Just exactly what did you do, Mac, to steam him up?"

Mac and Frank exchanged glances.

"I went out and looked in his shed to see if he had a deer. He had one, all right."

Mac was going to tell Sam about the bits of alfalfa hay that were found in the deer's carcass, but Frank almost imperceptibly shook his head and there was warning in his eyes.

"So, he was telling the truth," Sam said. "That's strange. He'd rather lie any day."

"Did you tell him it was me, Sam, and not you?"

"I didn't bother to," Sam said, and added dryly, "I didn't want to jeopardize the employer-employee relationship between you two."

"Did he ask you what you were looking for, Sam?" Frank asked.

"No. He just told me to keep the hell off his place."

"I wonder why he's so steamed up?" Frank asked, almost to himself.

"Sam, I can get you off the hook in short order," Mac said. "I've got a right to search premises for game. I can tell Chuck that, and I don't think he'd object."

"Let it lie, let it lie," Sam said easily. "It's not worth bothering about."

He straightened up and asked, "Anything in the depositions that interest you, Frank?"

"I'll tell you later," Frank said.

"Then so long, gentlemen," Sam murmured, and left the room.

When he was gone, Mac asked, "Why not

let Sam know about Chuck's deer, Frank?"

Frank growled, " 'Cause I haven't got this figured out in my own mind." He hesitated. "Does it strike you that Chuck might be worried about something. Could that explain his call to Sam?"

"You could read it that way. Or you could read it that he's just an ornery slob that was born resenting his betters."

At that moment they both looked up at a man who entered the room. He was an old-timer shabbily dressed in a World War I khaki-colored mackinaw and an old cap. Both men knew him as an old miner and a wino. His name was Tony Cuccinelli. As he walked haltingly toward the counter, they both said hello.

"I never thought I'd see you come in here when you weren't under arrest, Tony," Frank said. "You got troubles?"

Tony gave him a toothless grin and scratched his cheek, which held two weeks of pure white beard stubble. "Not my trouble," Tony said. "I'm looking for Minnie Gerber."

"Here?" Frank asked, puzzled.

"No. I mean she's gone. Her cats were howling all last night. No feed, I guess. She ain't home. No fire, water frozen, and cats hungry. Nobody around us has seen her for a couple of days."

232

"She could be visiting somewhere," Frank said.

"You visit and not turn off your water? You don't ask somebody to feed your cats?"

Frank sighed resignedly. "Okay, Tony. I'll have a look." He moved over to where his hat and jacket were hanging on the wall and said to Mac, "I don't know what to make of this puzzle you handed me, Mac. Something is missing. Leave that hay with me, will you?"

Mac said good-bye and left the courthouse. He got into his pick-up, started the motor, and turned up the heater, but he did not back out immediately. He watched Frank and Tony get into Frank's car and drive off. Something missing, Frank had said. What was missing was Chuck Daily's reason for coming back to town the morning Judge Lillard was killed.

Mac shook his head, put the car in gear, and backed out. He was going to try to find Chuck now and get the last load of wood hauled. If he could find Chuck, he would get a chance to finish his monthly report today. He turned down behind the courthouse and drove down the snowy road, his tires squealing against the dry snow.

Pulling up at Chuck's shack, he took the path up to the kitchen door. He had his hand raised to knock when he saw Chuck working on the shed door. Because his boots squeaked in the snow, Chuck had warning of his approach this time and turned around. Mac could see the gleam of a new hasp that Chuck was screwing into the wood. On the other half of the hasp a shiny new padlock hung, its keys dangling. Mac hauled up beside Chuck, who said, "Morning, Mac. Bet you're wondering where I went to?"

"I hoped you wouldn't quit with only one more load to go, Chuck."

"Oh, I ain't." He gestured toward the padlock. "I had to put this thing on so I could lock my shed, Mac. Damn kids are stealing my meat."

Mac looked at him searchingly, knowing he was lying. Unless the kids came in after his visit yesterday, Chuck's meat was intact. Mac knew that this was directly related to his visit yesterday, and further that there was something in the shed that Chuck wanted to hide.

"Finish up, Chuck. Then you can drop me off at the courthouse," Mac said.

Mac walked back to the car and got into the cab. It was only minutes before Chuck joined him. Driving back to the courthouse, both men were silent. When Mac stepped out, Chuck slid across the seat behind the wheel. Mac said, "I'll be home when you get in, Chuck, and you'll get your check."

Chuck nodded and drove off, and Mac walked toward the courthouse entrance. Then he halted and regarded the parked cars ranked in front of the courthouse. Frank's car was not there, and Mac knew it probably would not be for some time. He would be out rounding up his deputies. Still, with the knowledge that Chuck was hiding something in that shed and that he had lied about his meat being stolen, Mac had to think this out and talk it out. He wondered if Jessie was busy.

Cutting across the park, he went into Sam's office. Jessie was typing, but she stopped at Mac's entrance.

"You're very attentive today, my friend. Trying to make up for neglecting me?"

Mac grinned and sat down onto the sofa. "I'm lonesome," he said. "Is Sam around?"

"So, you're lonesome for Sam?" Jessie said tartly.

"No, I want to talk with you, but not if Sam is about to call you."

"He's out," Jessie said. "I'd love to talk to you. What shall we talk about?"

"Did Sam tell you about Chuck Daily's call to him last night?"

"He just got through telling me about it. You're the one who should have got the phone call, aren't you?"

Mac nodded, and now, feeling sudden impatience and restlessness, he rose and began to pace the floor. "Jessie, listen to a story, a true story," he said, and he saw her regarding him with curiosity.

"Is there a happy ending?"

"I wish I knew," Mac said. Then he told her about his visit to Chuck's shed and the discovery of wisps of alfalfa in the deer's carcass. He had not told her before about Cy Hartford's spotlighter, but he did now, mentioning also that the killing of the deer occurred on the night of opening day when Chuck Daily was in town.

As he slowly paced the floor, he was not so much talking to Jessie as thinking aloud, marshaling and emphasizing the salient points of Chuck Daily's strange behavior. He mentioned again what Jessie already knew — that Chuck had left his camp in good deer country to shoot a deer on Cy Hartford's for no explainable reason. He told of surprising Chuck chopping wood and of the terror that was momentarily reflected in Chuck's face. Then he told her of his visit to Chuck this morning and of finding him putting a padlock on the shed.

He finished by saying, "Jessie, there's something in that shed that Chuck wants to hide. That padlock wasn't put on to keep kids from stealing meat. All his meat was there yesterday afternoon. I'll swear it's there now. No, it's something he doesn't want anyone to see."

"You mean there's something he doesn't want Sam to see."

"Put it that way if you want," Mac said. "Now, what is it that Sam is most concerned about?"

As soon as he had asked this, he halted and looked at Jessie.

Jessie said, "What?"

"Why, the thing Sam's most concerned about is the death of his father. The only thing. That's another way of saying that he's concerned about finding the death weapon, the rifle that killed the Judge, isn't it?"

Jessie slowly nodded and now Mac walked up to her desk. "What else but the death weapon would Chuck Daily try to hide from Sam?"

Jessie shook her head. "But Mac, Chuck gave you his gun. It was a two-seventy and Frank says that it was a thirty-ought-six bullet that killed the Judge."

Mac felt a rising excitement as he said, "He could have had two guns, Jessie."

"With him?" Jessie asked swiftly.

"Oh, Lord!" Mac exclaimed vehemently. "Don't you see? This explains his trip to town on the morning of opening day. He wanted to get rid of the gun that killed the Judge."

Mac stood utterly motionless; his glance was on Jessie but his eyes were unseeing. "That explains the killing of that deer at Cy Hartford's or somewhere else. Chuck knew he would have to show a reason for leaving his camp."

Again Jessie shook her head. "Mac, if he killed the Judge, he'd have simply left the Officer's Creek country."

Mac pounced on that swiftly. "Oh no! He was seen coming in. Frank would have learned that he was there." Now Mac's usually slow and emotionless voice held a real excitement. "Don't you see, Jessie, it's been shouting at us and we haven't been listening! Lord knows why Chuck killed the Judge, but he did. He knew he'd be questioned and that his rifle would be tested. He knew he had to hide the rifle and substitute another one. He also knew that he'd be seen entering that area and would be questioned. He shot the deer at Cy's so he could show a reason for leaving his camp. He came back to the camp with a different caliber gun because he knew Frank would hunt him out eventually."

Jessie said dryly, "Mac, honey, you're dreaming."

"I'm not, I'm not!" Mac almost shouted. "It's the only thing that makes sense out of what we already know — the two sets of jeep tracks, the deer that had eaten hay, the deer that was shot at Cy's, the phone call to Sam, and the padlock. Can't you see that?"

Jessie said slowly, "Yes, but what was his motive?"

"The hell with his motive!" Mac said flatly.

"You have no proof that Chuck ever owned a thirty-ought-six."

"Maybe I can get proof."

"He was hunting alone," Jessie pointed out. "Somebody would have had to see him with a thirty-ought-six."

Mac turned, swept his hat from the sofa and put it on, then he looked at Jessie. "Hold tight, baby, give me ten minutes."

He hurried out, turned left, and almost ran the two blocks to Bartlett's Sporting Goods Shop. Bill Bartlett, a schoolmate of Mac's and almost as tall, was in the storeroom down cellar, the clerk informed Mac. Going down the wooden stairs, Mac found Bill unpacking ski boots. When Bill looked up and saw Mac, he grinned.

"I wondered when you'd be in for your hunting license, Mac." Bill wore horn-rimmed glasses whose lenses were as thick as plate glass, but Mac knew him for one of the best duck shots he'd ever seen.

Looking around the room which held the

rough shelves that housed much of Bill's inventory, Mac saw that they were alone.

"Bill, does Chuck Daily trade with you?" he asked abruptly.

Bill rose and scratched his head. "You wouldn't call it that exactly. I sell him a pair of boots every couple of years, gloves and socks too. Stuff like that."

"Sell him ammunition?"

"Yes, that too."

"Think hard now, Bill. When did you sell him ammunition last, and what caliber was it?"

Bill thought a moment. "He drops around every once in a while and picks up a couple of boxes of twenty-twos. I've sold him shells for a two-seventy, too." Mac felt a bitter disappointment, but then he saw Bill wasn't through. "A couple of days before opening day he came in and bought a box of thirty-ought-six shells."

Mac felt a wild exultation then and he asked, "You sure of that, Bill?"

Bill nodded. "I remember because Chuck wanted one-eighty grain shells. I'd been cleaned out of them and he had to settle for one-fifty. He was sort of halfway sore about it."

"You absolutely certain, Bill?" Mac persisted.

"If you mean would I take an oath on it, I would," Bill said. "What's so important about it?"

"We'll know in a few days, maybe sooner, Bill. Just keep this between us, will you?"

"If you say so."

Bill watched Mac go up the stairs two at a time and he wondered why Mac was in such a hurry that he couldn't chat or even say "so long."

Out in the cold wintery air, Mac headed back towards Sam's office and Jessie. He had almost reached it when he looked across the park and saw Frank's car nose into the curb. Changing his mind, he cut across the park, heading for Frank's office.

Frank was at his typewriter. He regarded Mac thoughtfully as he closed the door and snapped the lock.

"What's that for?" Frank asked.

Mac didn't answer immediately. He walked around the end of the counter, and without being invited took the chair beside Frank's desk.

"I just don't want to be interrupted, Frank." He paused, marshaling his facts. "After you threw me out of the office earlier, I drove to Chuck Daily's place to see if he'd haul my last load of wood. Guess what I found him doing?"

"Sleeping, probably."

"He was putting a padlock on his shed. He said the kids were stealing his meat. If they did, it had to be after four o'clock yesterday when I was there."

"Maybe he just doesn't like snoopers. That's his right."

"I don't think so," Mac said slowly. "I think he's hiding something in there and I think I know what it is." Mac hesitated. "I think he's hiding the thirty-ought-six that killed the Judge."

Jolted, Frank rose and looked down at Mac, a look of incredulity in his face. Then he said derisively. "You don't pay much attention to the printed word, do you? The caliber of Chuck's gun was two-seventy."

"Then why did he buy thirty-ought-six shells from Bill Bartlett a couple of days before the season opened?"

"Who said he did?" Frank demanded swiftly.

"I just came from talking with Bill. He said he'd take an oath on it that he sold Chuck a box of one-fifty grain thirty-ought-six shells."

"He could have bought them for somebody else, though that's not likely."

Mac slapped the desk with the palm of his hand. "Frank, it all fits in! Chuck knew his thirty-ought-six would eventually give him

242

away. He had to exchange it for his two-seventy. He knew you'd ask him why he left his camp. That explains Cy's deer; and because he had been seen going to the Officer's Creek country, he had to return. Everything fits in, Frank! Shoot a hole in it if you can!"

Frank took his characteristic stroll to the window, looked out at the snowy park, then he turned. "I can't, Mac. Also I can't figure out how you thought of it."

Mac said wryly, "By accident. I was talking to Jessie. She pointed out that it was really Sam and not me or the kids that Chuck was padlocking out. Why should Chuck think Sam was concerned with any possessions of his unless it related to the Judge's killing? It had to be the thirty-ought-six."

Frank said dryly, "If you hadn't borrowed Sam's car yesterday, we'd still be sweating this out."

"That's about it."

The sheriff leaned down to a shelf in the counter and drew out a blank warrant. As he filled it out, except for the signature, he asked, "When you figure Chuck will be back, Mac?"

"Oh, between noon and one." Both men looked at their watches and saw it was close to twelve o'clock.

"Having lunch with Jessie like always?"

243

Frank asked. When Mac nodded, Frank said, "Call her up and cancel out. I'll be needing you."

Mac reached for the phone, asking, "Do I tell her about the shells, Frank?"

"Tell her nothing until we've got that gun of Chuck's — if there is one."

Mac called Jessie at the office and the first thing she asked him was, "Where did you go, Mac? What did you find?"

"I'll tell you later, honey. Also, I can't make it for lunch."

"You wretch! You're up to something," Jessie said lightly. Then she almost whispered, "I can tell you're excited, Mac. Oh, make it good!" She hung up before Mac could answer.

When Mac finished with the phone, Frank took it and dialed a number. "Oscar," he said into the phone, "Stick around the store for a minute. I've got a warrant for you to sign."

Both men went out into the still cold noon and got in Frank's car. They drove around the square to the drug store owned by Oscar Landsman, who, as in many of the state's small towns, was both businessman and Justice of the Peace.

Frank was gone only a minute, and came out of the drug store tucking the warrant in his shirt pocket.

Back in the car, he asked, "Think Chuck will unload at your place first, or go home and get something to eat?"

"I couldn't guess, Frank."

"Where did you cut your wood?"

"Up above the old Tabor ranch."

Frank nodded and headed east out of town on the main highway. He drove at a leisurely pace, and several cars, some with deer roped to their fenders, passed them going the other way. Mac realized that in the last few days he had not even thought about hunting and hunters.

Presently Mac's green pick-up passed them. Chuck Daily spotted the red light on Frank's sedan and waved to him. Frank waved back. At the next side road he turned around and headed the other way, keeping the pick-up in sight. When the truck did not turn off on the river road, they knew Chuck was going to unload first.

Frank asked abruptly. "What's this shed of Chuck's like?"

"It's an old dirt-floored barn. Chuck's got some junk stored there in barrels."

When Frank pulled up in Mac's driveway, they could hear Chuck pitching out the wood before stacking it. Frank, ahead of Mac, rounded the corner of the garage into which the pick-up was halfway backed.

"Hello, Chuck," Frank said quietly. "I got something for you to read." He reached in his pocket and handed Chuck the warrant.

There was a puzzled look on Chuck's beard-stubbled face. He took off his tattered gloves and jammed them in the pocket of his filthy jacket before accepting the paper.

"What is it, Frank?"

"Read it."

Chuck stepped beyond the shadow of the pick-up for better light and studied the paper. Then he looked up almost immediately. "Search warrant?" he asked.

"If you'll read on, you'll see why."

Chuck didn't even look at the warrant, but only said. "Why?"

"Suspicion of possessing and concealing a murder weapon."

Chuck's glance shifted to Mac and then back to Frank.

"What murder weapon?"

Frank said quietly, "The thirty-ought-six that was used to murder Judge Lillard. Now leave your work, Chuck. Get in my car and we'll go to your house."

"I don't own a thirty-ought-six!" Chuck protested hotly. "I own a two-seventy. You saw it! You had it at your office!"

"Come along, Chuck," Frank said.

"You can't do this!" Chuck retorted angrily.

"I want a lawyer!"

"Afterwards, if you want one, Chuck. He can't do anything for you now." Frank moved over to him and touched his elbow. "Move along, Chuck."

Resignedly Chuck circled the pick-up and headed for Frank's car, with Frank trailing. Mac went over to the back wall of the shed where the tools were racked, and took down a shovel and pickaxe. By the time he reached Frank's car, Frank and Chuck were inside waiting.

Mac pitched the tools in the back seat, and climbed in.

As Frank pulled the car away, Chuck said in a whining voice, "You got this all wrong, Frank. I got a two-seventy and a twenty-two. That's all."

"Then you shouldn't object to my looking around, Chuck," Frank said quietly.

The rest of the trip was made in silence. When they pulled up at Chuck's place, Chuck and Mac climbed out. Frank waited until Chuck was circling the car before snapping open the glove compartment, from which he took a pair of handcuffs that he slipped in his pocket. Climbing out of the car, he fell in behind Chuck, while Mac with the tools brought up the rear.

When Chuck reached the back door, he

247

brought out his key to unlock it and said over his shoulder, "Every damn thing I've got is in here."

"Don't bother with your house, Chuck. It's the shed we want to search."

"There's nothing in the shed but meat and some junk!"

"Give us a look," Frank said.

Mac, even from some feet away, could see the sweat running down Chuck's forehead.

"Well, I've got to go in and get the padlock keys," Chuck said.

"I'll go with you," Frank said swiftly.

Mac, as he waited, knew that Frank was taking no chance of Chuck getting hold of one of his guns.

Moments later the three of them tramped down to the shed, where Chuck unlocked the shiny new padlock. Mac shoveled the snow away from the door so it could be opened wide for more light. Frank pushed the door back and then regarded the interior.

"You can see for yourself," Chuck said in a hurt tone. "There's nothing here but meat and junk."

"Roll those barrels over to the door, Chuck."

"Not me," Chuck said flatly. "I know what's in them. Why should I look again?"

"I'll do it, Frank," Mac said. He moved

past them, past the meat, tilted the first barrel and manhandled it to the door, where Frank tipped it over. It held Chuck's camping equipment, and old axe, a piece of tarp, and some rusty tin plates. By the time Mac had moved the second barrel, Frank was finished examining the contents of the first. The second barrel held mostly mice-gnawed blankets. The third barrel was almost empty and held nothing but empty tin cans and dirt.

When Frank was finished, Chuck said sarcastically, "Anything in them that looks like a thirty-ought-six?"

Frank, without answering, moved into the room and stood regarding it, hands on hips. Then he said, "Give me a shovel, Mac."

Mac handed it to him, wondering if they were going to have to dig up the whole floor. However, Frank up-ended the shovel and, beginning at the front wall, started tamping the floor with the shovel handle.

He would lift the shovel a foot or so in the air and bring the handle sharply down on the hard-packed dirt. It seemed uniformly hard as he moved toward the corner where the barrels had been. He moved a little farther into the room and started back on a parallel course.

Then suddenly the sound made by the shovel handle tamping the hard earth altered slightly. It was a duller sound and Mac saw the shovel handle sink a little deeper than it had before. Frank caught it too, for he tapped several times in the same spot. The dirt here was looser.

Now Frank switched ends of the shovel and began to dig. Mac, engrossed, momentarily forgot Chuck. Silently, Chuck had retreated to the pile of junk emptied from the barrel, and just as silently he extracted the old axe.

At that moment, Frank struck an object. He looked up, about to speak to Mac. Then he shouted, "Watch out, Mac!"

Mac wheeled in time to see Chuck, the axe raised above his head, charging him.

Mac knew instantly that if he backed off he would be overtaken by Chuck's down-driving axe. Then he did the only thing left him: he lunged toward Chuck and it took him under the down swing of the axe.

The two men met with a bone-jarring impact, and Mac, remembering his football days, wrapped his arms around Chuck's thighs, lifted him and kept driving.

His tackle drove Chuck back into the wall and Mac pinned him there long enough for Frank to wrench the axe, which Chuck was raising again, from his hands. Then Chuck struck out at Mac's head, hammering down at it with clenched fists. He was so intent on freeing himself, that he never saw Frank's driving left hand. The blow caught Chuck on his chin and his head rapped back against the wall. Then, almost gracefully, he slacked forward over Mac's shoulder, arms hanging down.

Mac straightened up and dumped him on the floor. Swiftly Frank took out the cuffs, rolled Chuck over, and handcuffed his hands behind his back.

Then Frank said, "I think I know what I hit with that shovel, Mac."

Both men were panting as they went back to the spot where Frank had dropped his shovel. In a matter of minutes, they had the tarp-wrapped 30.06 and shells lying on the floor before them.

Mac slowly moved over to Chuck and then he looked over his shoulder at Frank. "I'd like to kick his head off, Frank, but I don't think the Judge would have approved."

Chuck groaned and rolled over now, and Mac moved up to stand beside Frank.

"You're coming with me, Chuck," Frank said. "Stand up." He said over his shoulder to Mac, "Bring Chuck's rifle and the shells, will you, Mac?"

A short time later in Frank's office, Chuck, still handcuffed, was waiting in one of the chairs on the outside of the counter. While

Mac deposited the gun and shells on the counter, Frank called Sam's office. Mac heard him say, "Jessie, you and Sam get over here on the double. Bring your book. We've got a prisoner who's going to make a statement." He paused, "That's right," he said in answer to Jessie's question. Then he hung up.

Moving around the counter, Frank walked up to Chuck, halted, and put his hands on his hips. "Chuck, you've got a right to call a lawyer. But before you do, I'll tell you what's going to happen to you. You're under arrest on suspicion of murder, also for assault with intent to kill. On the first charge, I can hold you in jail for seventy-two hours. Your lawyer can get you out on bail on the second charge, but the seventy-two hours hold, come hell or high water." He paused, "Now listen carefully. I'm going to make a phone call and I want you to hear what I say."

Chuck's sullen face didn't alter as Frank turned and went over to the phone. From the basket on his desk he drew out the letter that contained the ballistics report, opened it, and laid it on the desk. Then he dialed the operator and when he had her, he said, "I want to place a person-to-person call to Mr. Charles Petrie. He's in the Ballistics Laboratory at the Washington office of the Federal Bureau of Investigation. I don't have the number, operator." He gave his own name and number.

There was a pause. Frank and Mac watched Chuck. He was sitting tense, ready to listen to what Frank was going to say. After a long wait, during which Jessie and Sam came into the room, Frank spoke into the phone. "Mr. Petrie, this is Sheriff Cosby in Ute City. D'you remember signing the ballistics report on the bullets from thirty-one rifles?" He paused. "Yes, that's right. I have another test bullet I'm air-mailing today to you personally. You should have it tomorrow morning. It's urgent that I have an immediate test. I'm holding a suspect, but only for seventy-two hours." Another pause. "Then you'll call me tomorrow night? Here's my number." Frank gave it to him, thanked him, and hung up.

Mac, meanwhile, had simply shaken his head in answer to Jessie's whispered questions. It was Frank's party, he thought, and he wanted to take away nothing from Frank's telling of what had happened.

Now Frank came from behind the counter and said to Sam as he put his hand on Chuck's rifle, "I think this is the gun that killed the Judge, Sam. We'll know tomorrow." He looked at Jessie, whom Mac was helping out of her coat. "Got your book, Jessie?"

"Right here."

Frank drew up a chair facing Chuck and

Jessie sat down. Frank stood beside her. "You heard the phone call, Chuck." Frank said. "Want to call a lawyer?"

Chuck shook his head. "What's the use?" he mumbled.

Frank pounced. "Then you must have a statement to make. I'll ask you right out. Did you kill Judge Lillard?"

"It was an accident," Chuck muttered. He would not look at any of them, but stared at his boots.

"The first shot, yes. The second shot, no. Did you fire the second shot into Judge Lillard's body?"

Chuck only nodded assent.

"Why?" Frank asked.

"He seen me and I reckon I lost my head. I figured with my record I'd spend years in jail. The Judge would see to that."

"So you shot him?" Frank demanded.

Chuck's answer was a nod.

Frank, Jessie, and Mac all looked at Sam at the same time. Sam's broad face was drained of color and in his dark eyes was a fathomless look of contempt. Not hatred — contempt. Mac wondered if he would speak, and if he spoke, what he could say.

Sam only picked up his hat, and without looking at any of them, went out the door and turned down the corridor.

THORNDIKE-MAGNA hopes you have enjoyed this Large Print book. All our Large Print titles are designed for easy reading, and all our books are made to last. Other Thorndike Press or Magna Print books are available at your library, through selected bookstores, or directly from the publishers. For more information about current and upcoming titles, please call or mail your name and address to:

THORNDIKE PRESS
P.O. Box 159
Thorndike, Maine 04986
(800) 223-6121
(207) 948-2962 (in Maine and Canada call collect)

or in the United Kingdom:

MAGNA PRINT BOOKS
Long Preston, Near Skipton
North Yorkshire,
England BD23 4ND
(07294) 225

There is no obligation, of course.